C   Mackay Brown (*1921–96*) was one of the twentieth
c   y's most distinguished and original writers. His lifelong
i   tion and birthplace, Stromness in Orkney, moulded his
       the world, though he studied in Edinburgh, and later
       _dwin Muir at Newbattle Abbey College. From 1941
c   vards he battled tuberculosis, and increasingly lived a re-
    :ve life in Stromness, but despite his poor health he
    !uced a regular stream of publications from 1954 onwards.
    s: included *Loaves and Fishes* (1959), *A Calendar of Love*
(.   i7), collections of short stories *A Time to Keep* (1969) and
1   vkfall (1974), a widely read novel *Greenvoe* (1972), *Time in a*
     Coat (1984) and a steady output of prose and poetry,
n   ibly the novel *Beside the Ocean of Time* (1994), which
v   shortlisted for the Booker Prize and winner of the Saltire
F   k of the Year. His work is permeated by the layers of history
i   :cotland's past, by quirks of human nature and religious
b   ef, and by a fascination with the world beyond the horizons
c   ie known.

       was honoured by the Open University and by Dundee
    !asgow Universities. The enduringly successful St Magnus
        of poetry, prose, music and drama held annually in
    y keeps his memory alive and is his lasting memorial.

OTHER TITLES BY GEORGE MACKAY BROWN

Novels
Beside the Ocean of Time
Greenvoe
Magnus
Vinland

Stories
A Calendar of Love
A Time to Keep
The Golden Bird
Hawkfall
The Island of the Women

Autobiography
For the Islands I Sing

GEORGE MACKAY BROWN

The Masked Fisherman and Other Stories

Polygon

This edition published in Great Britain in 2008 by
Polygon, an imprint of Birlinn Ltd
West Newington House
10 Newington Road
Edinburgh
EH9 1QS

www.birlinn.co.uk

ISBN 978 1 84697 084 9

First published in 1989 by John Murray (Publishers) Ltd

British Library Cataloguing-in-Publication Data
A catalogue record for this book is
available on request from the British Library.

Typeset by Hewer Text UK Ltd, Edinburgh
Printed in Great Britain by Clays Ltd, St Ives plc

To Brian Murray

Contents

Acknowledgements

'The Tree and the Harp' was first published in *A Quiver of Ghosts* edited by Aidan Chambers, The Bodley Head, (1987); 'Pace Eggs' (1982) and 'The Christmas Dove' (1981) in the *Tablet*; 'Anna's Boy' and 'Miss Tait, Tommy and the Carol Singers' (1984) on BBC Radio Orkney; 'The Corn and the Tares' (1987), 'The Nativity Bell and the Falconer' (1987) and 'The Weaver' (1987) in the *Glasgow Herald*; 'The Masked Fisherman' (1985), as a book entitled *The Hooded Fisherman*, by K. D. Duval and C. H. Hamilton; 'Sylvanus, A Monk of Eynhallow' (1984) on BBC Radio 3; 'Shore Dances' (1981) in *Temenos*; 'The Scholar' in *Scottish Short Stories 1982*, Collins with the Scottish Arts Council; 'A Haul of Winter Fish' (1983), 'Winter Song' (1980) and 'Dialogue at the Year's End' (1987) in the *Scotsman*; 'Christmas Visitors' in *Christmas Stories*, Perpetua Press, (1985); 'A Croft in January' (1988) on BBC Radio Scotland.

Introduction

Many of the stories in this book are set in winter, round about Solstice and Christmas and New Year.

In the north, winter has always been the time for story-telling. In Orkney until recently the hearth-fires were stoked up in Hall and croft on the long nights and story-tellers and fiddlers came into their own.

Winter, season of storm and dearth, is still a mighty quickener of the imagination. The stuff of narrative lies thick everywhere, but in the past rather than in the present. Now the mind is too easily satisfied with the withering pages of newspapers and their 'stories', and with the fleeting shallow images of television serials.

The medieval Icelanders were magnificent story-tellers. Their kinsmen in Orkney and Shetland had the *Orkneyinga Saga*, an anthology of stories to hold children from their play and enthral old men in chimney corners on a winter night. Those sagas were hewn from the inexhaustible quarry of human nature, as it appears in action and speech: vivid timeless masques. Real earls and heroes and villains bestride our saga, and the common people, as in Shakespeare and Sophocles, make rare appearances. I have chosen to elaborate one of the most moving incidents from the *Orkneyinga Saga*, in which the greatest of the Orkney earls, Rognvald Kolson, has dealings with fisher-folk in Shetland. The many-faceted character of the man – master of verse, navigator, statesman, as well as more homely skills – is flashed off this one exploit.

But the quarry for northern imaginative writers is deeper still. There were the older tribes that built the brochs, and Skara Brae and Brodgar; back and back to the first hewers and setters of stone, mysterious shadows on the skyline who came not too long after the melting of the ice. Those anonymous peoples have left only a few marks on their stones. Their languages are lost. Their stories perhaps survive in the remaining fragments of folk-lore.

The wheel of summer light and winter darkness must always have influenced northern poets and story-tellers: their themes and styles. The seasons are not opposites, but complementary. It is in winter barns and cupboards that the riches of summer are stored. Into the dark solstice comes the light of the world. We know that our candles and fires are one with the corn-ripening sun. From the wheel of the year came, wavering and lovely, the dances of Johnsmas in summer and the boisterous Yuletide reels.

A northern story-teller must try to order his words into the same kind of celebration.

G.M.B.
December 1988

The Eve of St Thomas

1

The man woke up in his hut, and he heard the wind prowling outside. Through the small window of his bothy he could see the dark clouds moving swiftly, high up. A little grey light entered.

Very faintly, he could hear the dash of waves against the headland.

Ah well, there would be no fishing on such a day. He was glad about that. Half a dozen of the young men had spent the night before up at the smithy, drinking the blacksmith's grey whisky, a month old. It was said to be a very good whisky, the best in the island, the best in all Orkney maybe. And it was Thomas the blacksmith's special winter brew. This young fisherman did not like it, but if he had refused to go up to the shuttered smithy on the night of the tasting of the winter brew, he would be shamed forever in the parish. The young ploughmen wouldn't want to be seen speaking to him till after the year was on the turn. This fisherman was a good-natured man, and well-liked everywhere. It would be a sorrow to him to be denied the friendship of his fellow bachelors, even for a day or two.

Next winter it would be different. In June he would be married to Norda, and then he would be no longer expected to have a first taste of the awful new home-distilled whisky up at the blacksmith's. A married man was not wanted on those occasions.

Ah well, he had gone up to taste the winter whisky at the smithy – and he knew well what the outcome would be – and now he lay here in his bed, with misery in his head and stomach, and lead in his bones.

He couldn't remember much of the celebration either, after the first hour. There had been a chorus or two, and Jock of the Mill had tried to tell a ghost story but had forgotten the end, and that had brought on him a storm of derision. And all the time the bowl of grey rank stuff had gone round, replenished now and then from the great tilted stone jar of Thomas the blacksmith.

How the young island men had teased each other, awkwardly and gently to begin with!

Even though he took only small sips out of the circling bowl, the raw whisky made his throat wince. And his stomach burned, as if rags were smouldering there.

All at once, it seemed, he remembered little more of the night's drinking. He remembered, vaguely, that there had been a fight, two young men from rival farms raging about each other with tangled arms and strenuous shoulders, and the blacksmith tearing them apart. And he remembered Dod the fisherman from the Voe slithering off the bench and being carried over and laid down beside the forge. He remembered, dreamily, Will the orra-boy at the Glebe letting the bowl half full of whisky fall from his hands with first a splash and then the shattering of the bowl in a hundred clay shards. He remembered, quite distinctly, the drunken lad fumbling with the bowl, and the slow descent of a sheet of grey whisky on to the flagstone, and the fine curve the bowl made as it followed the liquor, and the faraway splash and the fine clean crisp crash . . . After that he remembered nothing.

Somehow he had found his way back through the midnight to the bothy. He was sure that no one had carried him home. That would have been a shame past bearing. He wondered, through his hangover, at the perils of his mile-long stagger between the smithy and his hut. The last two hundred yards was a narrow twisting track down the sea-banks.

It was well past noon. In two hours the sun would be down.

The storm would come to nothing. Already the sky westward was shredding thin, and the sun shone weakly through. The wind had shifted to the south now. The sea was quieter in the bay.

Tomorrow he could set his creels. He would *have* to set his creels, for more than a few shillings would have to be scraped together for the wedding in June. Tomorrow was the shortest day – after that the tides of light would begin to flow.

This bothy at the Taing that his great-grandfather had built was going to be pulled down, or burnt, and he and half a dozen other young men were going to build a proper house of quarried stone. And there he would bring Norda his young wife.

He threw off the blanket and heaved his wretched flesh-and-blood-and-bones on to the edge of the bed. He had slept in his clothes, but some very old instinct of propriety had made him take off his leather sea-boots, drunk as he was.

The mackerel bait was there in the jar. The creels, fifty of them, were neatly stacked in the corner next the sea.

Would he get them all baited before the sun went down? He would have to – it would be today an enormous pain-racked labour – he could not work in the darkness, and he had forgotten to put fish-oil in the lamp.

He took down the first creel, and then looked for the knife to cut the bait. What should have been the simplest of tasks called, this day, for courage and concentration.

A voice from the open door said, 'What thinks thu thu're doing, man?'

It was Norda, of course. 'What do you think I'm doing?' he said. 'What does it look like? I'm trying to do my work so that we can be married in summer' . . .

Norda took the knife out of his heavy hand.

'It's a good thing,' she said, 'that I came when I did. Do you not know what day this is?'

'It's the day after the winter whisky drinking,' he said. 'I'm suffering because of it.'

'The morn's Thomasmas Day,' said Norda. 'Nobody works on Thomasmas Day. If thu had baited one creel, man, something pitiful and cruel would have happened to thee. Thu may be sure of that. There would be no wedding next June, and no house built, and I'd end up a poor old withered woman in the black croft of Byres up there on the side of the hill.'

'That's all nonsense,' said the young fisherman. 'Time all that superstition was forgotten.'

But he put the knife back on the table, and stacked the creel once more.

'What fools men are!' she said. 'They all hate that coarse whisky the blacksmith makes. And yet they *must* take part in it, to show what fine manly chaps they are . . . Look at the way thee hand's shaking! Thu'd have cut thee fingers off. But that would be nothing to the worse things that would happen. Go back to thee bed, man. Look, I've brought thee some fresh milk. I knew it would be like this with thee. All the parish women knew what was going on in the smithy last night. The milk'll lie kind on thee stomach. Here's some lamp oil too, in this flask.'

He crawled back into bed as sore as if he had fought with a whale all night.

'It's kind and good wisdom we have from the folk that have been in the kirkyard for hundreds of years,' said Norda.

The sun through the webbed window was setting in a red and black smoulder, close to its southern meridian.

She smoothed the dark sweat-tightened curls of his hair and beard. This man Aaron Rolfson was to be the provider of their children. But the labour of every man is a chancy thing, and it is best always to hold carefully the old customs and ceremonies of the folk. In the strictness of the observance there is a sweetness and a release.

After the girl had lit the lamp – for now the midwinter shadows were gathering swiftly – she sat on the edge of the bed and sang to him:

> The very babe unborn
> Cries 'Oh, dule! dule!'
> For the breaking o' Tammasmas night
> Five nights afore Yule.

The words fell, like soothest drops, into his bruised ear.

2

For more than a year the man had known himself to be drained of ideas and images. He had been able to do nothing at his 'work of words'.

'I'll go back to my sources,' he said. 'That may unlock something.'

His roots lay in an island in the far north. He had never seen the place. All he knew were the few stories a grandfather had told him when he was very young. And his grandfather had left Orkney as a child, when his own father the seaman settled in Leith. But the power and the strangeness of the stories had remained with him always. In time he became a story-teller himself, a moderately successful author of adventure stories, spy stories, sophisticated thrillers. He had won a certain fame that he knew would go out, and never be rekindled, after his death. Several of his novels had been made into films. Financially, he was well off. There was no necessity for him to write another page, ever.

But the idleness and the impotence irked him increasingly.

He bought a copy of a new translation of the saga of the islands: a marvellous account of the medieval Norse earls of Orkney and their friends and enemies, their viking exploits, their bouts of piety, their winter burnings, their shifting relationships with the great king of Norway in the east. 'If only I could write as lithely and powerfully as that old nameless story-teller.'

It was getting on for midwinter. 'We are going north to the islands,' he told his wife. 'I think I may be able to pick up a thread or two again. It is just possible.'

Everything went wrong from the start. There was fog – the planes were delayed for two days. They lingered in Kirkwall. He visited the Norse Cathedral of Saint Magnus.

They waited in a draughty shelter at a village pier for the ferry to take them to the island. It was a stormy crossing. His wife wasn't sick, but among the spindrift and the plungings and the broken circles of gulls she gave him one look of utter misery and reproach.

The island of his ancestors, when he stepped ashore, was far from welcoming. A cold rain stung their faces.

The little hotel was one of those modern buildings that can be seen anywhere in the world, synthetic walls hastily bolted together. Except for the young proprietor and his wife, it was empty. 'You see, sir,' she said at the desk, 'we don't expect visitors in winter. The staff leave at the end of September' . . .

The room was bitterly cold. He had to put coins in a meter before the bars of a little electric fire began to glow.

He went out alone into wind and rain. Desolation and ugliness all around. Most of the crofts were in ruins. A few sheep moved on the hill. A dog barked distantly.

According to the sailor grandfather, the great place for stories had been the blacksmith's in the village. He met a boy on the road. With quick courtesy, the boy pointed to the road that led to the village. He came to it at last, a cluster of a dozen houses at a crossroads, a bleak old church, a shop that called itself a 'general merchant's' . . . In the shop which was also the post office he bought tobacco and asked where he might find the smithy. 'No,' said the apple-cheeked wife, 'there's been no smithy there for twenty years and more. The smithy got run down, you know, once the tractors took over from the work-horses. That's the building over there across the road, it's a garage now. The blacksmith's grandson, he runs it, if ever you need a taxi . . . This weather, it's awful! I hope it improves for you' . . .

His wife was in bed, reading, when he got back to the hotel. 'Did you find what you were looking for?' she said.

'Not yet,' he said.

He went to the bar. It was deserted and the shutter was up. He rang the bell. The young hotelier came. He asked for a double whisky.

The sun was down. Shadow by black shadow, the stormy greyness of the short winter day was being quenched. His family archaeology would have to wait till tomorrow. The young hotelier was English. He knew nothing about the island families.

'There's a house on the island called Taing,' the man said. 'Would you know where it is?'

'I'm sorry, sir,' said the hotelier. 'We've only been in the island a year.'

In the bar, over another large whisky, he turned the pages of the paperback *Orkneyinga Saga*. There were magnificent winter stories in it.

He closed the book and looked through the window. It was black dark outside, though it was only half-past five. The wind had torn the clouds apart. A few stars shone through the rent. His spirit stirred inside him. A faint glimmer of starlight moved on the turbulence of the sea.

'Would you be wanting anything more?' said the hotelier.

The writer and his wife ate a supper that came mostly out of tins. The chef had left at the beginning of winter, too.

They hardly spoke to each other. He had never seen such coldness of reproach on that lovely face.

He liked the woman who kept the shop. Next morning she wondered, aloud, over the purchase of tobacco, why on earth anybody would be wanting to come to the island at this time of year. Would he be a birdwatcher? The folk who dug up the old mounds and stones, they came at any old time. She wouldn't wonder if it wasn't government business that took him north. Or something to do with the nuclear energy or the oil.

'Are there any Rolfsons in the island nowadays?' he said. 'That's my name. I'm looking for places connected with my family.'

Well, if that wasn't a wonder! Of course lots of folk came to the island looking for their ancestors, generally in summer when the weather was good. Every summer there were five or six lots of Americans looking for 'their roots' – that's what they called the old ruined ruckles of crofts their ancestors had emigrated from . . . She had heard tell of the Rolfsons. But no, there were no Rolfsons in the island now – not one – only them in the kirkyard . . . Oh, it had been a great pleasure, talking to him. She hoped the weather would improve. But it was winter, near the shortest day. Some of the older men might be able to help him. Old Tom Skaill at Ness, he had a long memory now. Old Tom could go ranging back through the generations.

The church was locked. He read on the notice-board that a service took place there now every third Sunday, there being only one minister now for this and two other islands.

He wandered through the stone labyrinth of the dead and came at last to the corner where the Rolfsons lay. There were two or three Rolfson tombstones, but the one that interested him was carved with the names of his direct ancestors.

AARON ROLFSON, Fisherman
   born 1841 died 1875

NORDA ROLFSON, his wife
   born 1844 died 1924

WILLIAM ROLFSON, their son
   crofter and fisherman
   at Taing in this parish
   Born 1865 died a
   bachelor 1947

JESSIE ANN ROLFSON, their
   daughter. For many years
   servant at the Manse here
   Born 1867 died unmarried
   1920

SIGURD ROLFSON, their son,
   ships officer Born 1870 Lost
   with all the crew of SS
   Matilda that sank in a storm
   off the Norwegian coast near
   Trömso on 17 December 1912
   He has no known grave

There were a few other inscriptions for Rolfson children who had died in infancy. There it was, a whole family chronicle on two slabs of sandstone.

What interested him was the information about Sigurd Rolfson. Sigurd Rolfson had been his great-grandfather. His Leith grandfather, Sigurd's son, had hardly mentioned his own drowned father, though he had a whole rich anthology of sea reminiscences. Perhaps it was too painful a childhood memory. Perhaps it was bad luck to dwell on such things. Interrogated by the child, the old man would say, 'Ah, he was lost at sea, a long time ago it was,' and immediately veer off to other seamen and other memories that had the live sting of salt in them.

The sun was setting over the open sea when he left the kirkyard. It had been above the horizon for only a few hours. It was getting on now for the winter solstice. The storm of the last day or two had blown itself out. The air was cold and darkling and still. He saw for the first time that the island of his ancestors was beautiful; it had a cold austere beauty that moved him more profoundly than the warm fruitful islands where he and his wife spent much of their winters.

A dark cloud along the horizon received the sunken sun. He had the image of a great northern king on his death-bed: a Hakon or an Olaf.

As he entered the hotel, the young proprietor was waiting for him. 'Mrs Rolfson left with the ferry two hours ago, sir. Of course you'll know that. She left this note.'

In his icebox of a room he read the note: 'I couldn't take any more of it. I have done it this way so as not to hurt you. Don't worry about me, I have booked a plane for Glasgow that leaves at 4 o'clock. I hope you find what you are looking for. I still love you' . . .

He had done wrong, of course, to drag her deeper into their winter. She was a woman who loved laughter and sunlight and wine. Childless, and voluntarily childless, the first sere and yellow leaf was on her now. A fruitless tree withers fast.

A few local men came into the hotel bar that evening. He sat over by the window and turned the pages of the Saga and drank his whisky. The island men would look across at him from time to time. They were wondering about him, trying to place him. They were too shy to approach him. The time had not yet come for him to talk to them.

Before he went to bed he stood outside and looked at the night. The stars hung in magnificent clusters, his eyes could probe the gulfs and wells, 'lovely asunder starlight'. The sea moved gently against the shores and the crags.

He had a long dreamless sleep.

The next morning after breakfast he set out to look for the old man in the croft of Ness. The shop-woman gave him lucid directions. It was a fine day, cold and clear. The long laterals of hill and farmland and loch and moor were (he thought) like good classical prose. He had the feeling that the bare landscape would, dowered with the gold of summer, be transmuted to poetry.

The old crofter Tom Skaill was expecting him. 'The whole island kens you're a Rolfson, man. Do you think Jemima at the shop keeps secrets? The whole island knew before sunset, the day before yesterday, that a Rolfson had come back to claim some land or property – That's the general impression – "What else could bring him to the place?" '

'My great-grandfather was born in this island,' he said, 'at a place called Taing. His name was Sigurd Rolfson. He was a sailor and he was drowned off Norway in 1912. He left this island for Leith when he got married. He brought up his family there, five children. My grandfather, John Rolfson, was his eldest son. He was a sailor too. He died in his bed, gently enough, ten years ago.'

'I remember John Rolfson a little,' said Tom Skaill. 'He came to the island for his holidays, when he was a boy. We picked shellfish together out of the pools, on the shore below Taing.'

'I'd be more than glad to see Taing,' he said.

'There's not much to look at,' said the old man. 'It was a well-built house, Taing. But it's stood empty for twenty years and more. Come with me, Mr Rolfson. It's in a fold of the crags, Taing. You'd never find it by yourself.'

They walked together a mile along the shore. 'I've tried to read one or two of your books,' said Tom Skaill. 'They were beyond me, I had to put them down. Your things on television too – I did give them a trial, but I always switched them off long before the end.'

'They're trash,' said the visitor. 'You did well to pack them in.'

They laughed together, in the cold light. The sun sank into the sea, in the south-west. Its treasury was all but spent. Its fires gave no warmth.

The cottage built by Aaron Rolfson for his bride Norda was suddenly there. It had been built so strongly that the flagstone roof was intact still. Of the two windows, one was a vacant square. The other window of six small panes was unbroken, but for one crack. The old man thrust at the warped door. It opened, and they went inside.

Bleakness everywhere. That a family of seven children could have been reared in such a place, in two small rooms! Yet the essential things were there: the hearthstone, the niche for the water buckets and the niche for the lamp and the window recess for the Bible and for the jar of wild-flowers in summer. And the cupboard for the jars of salt and fish-oil and ale and honey and milk – indeed a few stone jars still lay about the floor. The old man pointed to the hooks in the ceiling where the sides of bacon would have hung in the winter. But the wooden box-bed that would have divided the house into two rooms was not there. 'Burnt for firewood,' said the old man. 'The young folk called flower-people used to stay here ten years ago, and move on. Nice enough young folk with guitars and long hair, from the cities. They haven't been coming this while.'

All that Rolfson the writer felt now was a slight glow of shame. The ancestors had spent their days in a poor place, and worked hard, without benefit of literature or art or music, and in time had withered into age and death. Yet their lives had been fruitful. Their lives had been rounded with meaning and an austere beauty. Whereas he had given nothing of any real worth to the world, and there was little he couldn't buy with his badly-earned wealth.

With a peatfire going, and the lamp burning in the window, and children's laughter, it would have been a happy enough place at this time of year, a century ago.

The sun was down. The cottage was beginning to fill up with shadows.

'I'm obliged to you,' said Rolfson, as he climbed up the narrow track to the road above.

'Look,' said Tom Skaill, pointing to a shelving rock below. Rolfson could just make out, in the gloom, a thick curve of wood.

'That's a keel,' said Tom Skaill, 'all that's left of the *Kestrel*. I've heard that it was old Aaron Rolfson himself that built the fishing boat. He died when he was a young man. They say he was hauling the *Kestrel* ashore, with baskets of fish in her. He was a very strong man, I've heard. He stumbled, and fell among the rocks. His wife was called Norda. I've heard this too, she was the bonniest woman in this island in her day. When Norda got to the fisherman, he was dead. He must have overtaxed his heart.'

'The pity of it,' said Rolfson.

'A good way to go, if you ask me,' said Tom Skaill. 'Who wants to flicker out among wheezings and white hairs, a nuisance to everybody? I've lived too long as it is, myself.'

'It has a certain beauty in it,' said Rolfson.

'They all had to do with the sea, the Rolfsons,' said Tom Skaill. 'Sailors and fishermen. One of them didn't go to sea – that was Sam Rolfson – I went to school with him – he was a lighthouse keeper. But lightkeeping has to do with the sea too, in a way.'

'I am the disgrace,' said Rolfson. 'Those books and scripts – what kind of tawdry voyages I've made in those works you rejected – and with justice, my good old friend.'

At the crossroads, he offered Tom Skaill a ten-pound note. Tom Skaill refused it, neither shy nor offended.

'Come and see me whenever you want,' he said. 'You can bring a dram – I'll take that from you.'

When he got back to the hotel, the hotelier was waiting for him. 'A word with you, sir. Could you give me some rough idea as to how long you'll be staying?'

'When I've found what I'm looking for,' said Rolfson. 'I don't know. Maybe a week or ten days yet.'

'It's going to be difficult, sir. You see, my wife and I are going away over Christmas. We're getting somebody in to look after the bar. We'll be closing up the rest of the hotel.'

'That's be all right,' said Rolfson. 'Just make out my bill and I'll leave at once.'

'You won't get a ferry back tonight, sir.'

'I'm not leaving the island.'

'There are one or two bed and breakfast places. But they mightn't be willing to have a guest at this time of year. Parties, family gatherings – you know how it is, near Christmas.'

'I have a place to go to.'

'That's all right then, sir. Supper will be ready in half-an-hour.'

'I'm leaving now.'

There was a half-moon, crescent. By its light he managed to get down the sea path to the half-ruined cottage, carrying his case.

Here, where his ancestors had been born and lived and died, he would spend the night.

Inside, it was bitterly cold. The faint radiance of the moon came through the window. The last smoulder of sunset faded. He noted the place: it was where the Atlantic horizon crossed the upright of the third pane to the right.

He spread his dressing gown over the stone floor, and lay down, and drew his coat over him.

The hours passed. He couldn't sleep. He imagined an Innuit story-teller would be much more comfortable in his snow-house than he was here.

Near midnight he got up, and stamped and threshed his blood into some kind of movement. He went outside. The night sky was magnificent, a purple-black field sown with stars. In the north, as he looked, it was as if bales of silk were being flaunted, silken folds and hangings flickered along the sky, green and white and yellow. He thought he could almost hear the rustling of that winter bazaar. It must be that the coldness had roused those hallucinations. Then he knew that he was looking at something he had never seen before, the aurora borealis.

He went down to the rock and touched the powerful keel of *Kestrel*.

Then he went back to the cottage and pulled the coat over himself. He was as far from sleep as ever. Certain episodes and images and enigmas he riddled over and over again in his mind. 'Here I am, on the longest night of the year, the most wretched man in this island.' This bleak thought cheered him faintly, because there was a certain justice in his situation. 'Here I lie, moderately wealthy, I could I suppose buy the whole island if I wanted to, and I lie here risking death – inviting death, almost – in a hovel!' The thought returned again and again to the reason for his coming. His writing had dried up. He had done nothing for more than a year. He had had the obscure impulse to return. If he could unblock the sources, then all might be well again, the stories for which he was famous would begin to flow once more. The night passed. One by one, fragments of those well-known thrillers surfaced. 'Deep psychological insight' . . . 'A master of suspense' . . . 'Powerful parables for our time' . . . Such things certain reviewers and critics had said. He was filled with slow disgust and resentment as the hollow characters and contrived situations of his novels heaved like jetsam through his mind. The stars through the window pierced him. He would never write in that way again. As he curled up tightly on the floor, under his expensive coat, it occurred to him that his gift – if he had any – must be turned in a new direction. It was not his gift only, it belonged to all the people, he was merely the helmsman who ought to be taking the treasures (if there were any) to the place they were destined for – a rich mysterious place, that could exist without them, but unless an artist, or indeed any person, brought his gifts to that shore, his hitherings and thitherings and hucksterings were void and meaningless. He was bound to the icy wheel of the stars. The night passed. The ache in his mind was more intense than the ache in his body.

There were small assertions and certainties, in the midst of his sea of wretchedness: a bellbuoy in the darkness, a light on a reef. He knew, more strongly than he had ever known, that he had indeed certain talents and gifts. They would declare themselves, sooner or later. He would, if he came out of this midwinter cave alive, find his true direction.

He slept. He had a few confused dreams of winged helmets, fires and blood, a candle in a quiet niche, a low chant.

When he woke, the light of morning was in the cottage.

He lay awhile. He felt sleepy and comfortable now. When he looked at his hands, they were blue. He couldn't feel his fingers. His legs were like blocks of wood. Life had withdrawn to the small fire-stone at the centre of his body.

He got up painfully, and put on his coat.

Tom Skaill was having his breakfast. He opened the door to Rolfson. 'Come in, man,' he said. 'There's tea in the pot. You can sit over there by the fire.'

Rolfson told him how he had passed the night.

'Well, well,' said the old man. 'You'd have been more comfortable here. But I suppose a man does what he wants to do. I think you'd be better biding here tonight. There's a bed in the next room.'

Rolfson said he would spend a few more nights in Taing. There was driftwood on the shore. He would have a fire. perhaps Tom would lend him a bucket and an old pot. He would buy a few tins of meat and fish in the shop, and potatoes. A fresh-water stream fell down the crag near Taing, where he could fill a stone jar.

'As you like,' said Tom Skaill. 'Have another cup of tea.'

The winter island fascinated him. He wandered here and there among the fields, along the shore where seals and cormorants were, up the small hill where a kestrel hung. The sun went in a cold shallow arc, low in the southern sky. A man here and there waved to him from byre-door or field. He recognized the drinkers from the hotel bar.

The postmistress-shopkeeper was astonished. 'Left the hotel, Mr Rolfson? Doing for yourself? I didn't know there were cottages to let. Where about? I have very good free-range eggs. A box of candles. Three pounds of potatoes. This loaf is from the bakehouse in Kirkwall. That will be three pounds forty-five pence. The tins of mince and beans are on offer.'

He left the shop without telling her where he was staying. It was more than likely that she knew already.

Tom Skaill had given him newspaper kindling. The drift-wood was dry. He ate the potatoes and mince out of the pot, almost burning his tongue. It was a good meal. He wiped the bottom of the pot with dry bread, and ate it too.

The sun was setting. It was just after three in the after-noon. The old dying head lay among the waves. The sunset embers glowed almost exactly on the same grid of window-frame and sea-line as on the afternoon before. The death of the sea-king was a long drawn-out thing.

He lit three candles, and read in the *Orkneyinga Saga* the pilgrimage of Earl Rognvald Kolson eight hundred years ago;

and the siege of a tyrant's castle in Spain; and how the bishop forbade an assault until after Twelfth Night.

Beside the sputtering sea-wood fire, under the two blankets Tom Skaill had lent him, he slept without dreaming for twelve hours.

He woke before dawn, and lit a candle, and drank a little cold water out of the jug.

He found his way down to the shore carefully in the darkness. The sky was thick with stars, but in the south-east there was a slow paling, and soon a welling of saffron and pink, then the fountain of light grew and the sun rose, a pure pristine orb as if it had been new-moulded. He thought of Blake and the heavenly host crying *Glory!* but his imagination would not take him that far.

He looked at his digital watch. The date was the twenty-third of December. The winter solstice was over.

A bright glittering mantle was thrown over the sea from horizon to shore. He moved over to the keel of his great-great-grandfather's yawl. The light came dazzling out of a rockpool below. His frail hand went over the powerful keel. Fitted with timbers and mast and rudder, the *Kestrel* would still be capable of a journey.

Rolfson walked across the fields to Tom Skaill's cottage. The chimney smoked. The old man rose early. He was at the table, eating his egg and bannock. He topped up his mug with tea and poured another mug for Rolfson.

Yes, Rolfson assured him, he hadn't slept so well for years. Nor eaten such a good supper either, nor enjoyed a fire so much as the smoke and crackle and flames of that smashed-up driftwood. He hadn't known that candle-light could be so beautiful.

Tom Skaill said he must go out and see to his few sheep. His guest was welcome to stay. Let him see that the fire didn't go out. 'Peats are in that basket against the wall.'

There must have been a hundred books on the varnished bookcase on the far side of the fire. The thought of books gave him a faint nausea, but his eye was compelled to the titles. He picked out a book on 'the calendar customs' of Orkney and Shetland. Where his finger lay, on the December chapter, he read

> The very babe unborn
> Cries 'Oh, dule! dule!
> For the breaking o' Tammasmas night
> Five nights before Yule.

Why, he wondered, should the longest night of the year be called after Thomas the doubter? Perhaps because Thomas had been the apostle who had held out longest against the certainty of life-out-of-death. He, of the twelve, had endured the longest darkness. At last, it was St Thomas who had voyaged farthest east of all the apostles, nearest to the sources of light, even (some said) as far as India.

Rolfson looked at himself in the mirror over Tom Skaill's wash basin. His face was filthy and stubbled gold-and-silver.

He put a peat on Tom Skaill's stove and went back to Taing. A man should be as clean as he could make himself to welcome the new light. He flung his clothes over a rock, and walked out into the rising tide. One huge bitter spasm whelmed him and drove the breath from his lungs. He turned and ran back to the cottage, his head streaming. He shook like a struck bell. He dried himself with the hand-towel from his case. He put on a clean shirt and clean socks. He shook his head like a dog; salt drops scattered over the flagstones.

Quaking still with the cold of the winter sea, he managed to set and light the fire. He remembered the whisky flask in his case. That would be very welcome now. But no: he would drink it with the old man, later.

He smashed more driftwood over his knee and fed the flames.

Now he stretched out and fell asleep beside the waves of warmth coming from the hearth. He dreamed of a navigator on a dark stormy sea, freighted with an unknown cargo, bound for a destination unknown.

He woke just before sunset. He noted that the sun, this afternoon, entered the sea just north of the grid of its setting on the previous day.

There could be no doubt about it. The tide of darkness had reached its ultimate ebb. Light was beginning to return to the north.

That night he and Tom Skaill drank whisky together at the fireside of Ness. The old man told as many stories of the Rolfsons as he remembered – of ancestors and cousins – of quarrels and alliances, small triumphs and tragedies – and a motley patchwork it was, 'of night and light and the half-light'.

Going home, he could see in the windows of a farm here and there little lighted Christmas trees. In the village the shop was bright, door and windows. The shop too had its tinsel tree. Miss Logan the shopkeeper was doing good business with late customers. There were a half dozen or so children spattering coins on the counter, wanting apples and sweets and mandarins wrapped in gold foil. One carried a tin whistle.

'You kids, be quiet!' cried the shopkeeper. 'Wait till I serve Mr Rolfson.'

Rolfson bought a cheap writing-pad and a box of candles and an ounce of tobacco and a half-bottle of whisky.

As he left the shop, a small boy cried, 'That's the funny man that's living in the ruin!'

The sketch of the fable he must write now – a long tale of a kind utterly new to him – filled his mind suddenly like an illumination. He lit the three candles quickly. The room was cold but there was no time to light the fire. He wrote the sketch down in the writing-pad, and the images came in an ordered solemn sequence, as if they had been waiting for a summoning bell. His pen stumbled across the paper with the urgency of their procession.

The winter tribute. It is time to go with the
        islands' tribute.
At the end of November
We set the keel for Norway, a lantern in the stern.
And had fair passage. And anchored in a fjord.
I knocked at the lodge of the castle.
A long gargoyle face – *The king is sick.*
A princess said, in the hall
Winter will be long – there is no heir – What are
        we but icemaidens after today?
There entered the king's room soon
The seven with hoods over their faces.
Eat below with the horsemen, I was told.
'The treasurer?' The treasurer could not be lured
        from the hoard, as if
        locked gold was the
        king's breath and blood.
A black bell shivered, once, in the tower.
The horsemen diced with blue fingers in the stable.
A girl put cinders in her hair.
The hooded seven
Stood round the last candle. One stood in the
        chapel, holding back
        his hood, in a rush of

> grey breath he quenched
>   the flame.
> They went down.
> They carried torches and the sword with runes on it,
>   to a ship.
> *The soul of the king will set out northwards, alone,*
>   *at midnight.*
> Peasants and fishermen
> Stood, red and black, at the edge of the circle of burning.
> In the shadows, unmoving, the very poor.
> The Orkney ship was twelve days out of the harbour.
> Where should I leave
> The gold and the jar and the poem I had carried
>   from the west?

He looked at the shape of the writing on the page. It was in the form of a poem, one of those modern poems that have cast off the shackles of rhyme and metre and obey some inner laws of incantation as strict and as compelling, and more truthful perhaps to the pulse of modern life.

No friendly critic had ever detected poetry in his tales. This was surely the first sketch of the architect; he would build upon it what his skills had prepared him for over two decades, he would write a long novel of mystery and espionage of the kind his large readership demanded; but set in the darkness of a thousand years ago.

In the new Dark Age that was about to come, the fable might be prophetic of a time a thousand years hence. He himself had little hope now that the moral impulses of mankind could contain the Faustian fires that had been invoked four centuries ago.

He read the few words again. They pulsed on the page like

a star. It would be wrong to touch them. He had done what he had never believed possible, written a poem.

The story-teller in him – the fame-seeker – sneered, 'Poetry – What do you know about poetry? Go home, get back to the libraries, man. You have a long research to do. This venture into legend will cost you much hard work. And all the time you'll be skirting the edge of disaster.'

Rolfson said, setting a match to the fire, 'Let it be what it is, then, a star in the night, a little poem for Christmas.'

He heard a scatter of small thin cold voices outside.

> God rest you merry, gentlemen,
> Let nothing you dismay.
> Remember Christ our saviour
> Was born on Christmas day
> To save us all from Satan's power
> When we were gone astray.
> O tidings of comfort and joy . . .

The children he had seen in the village store were standing in a group at the door. One held a lantern. Their mouths smoked in the frosty air. Their voices were as fragile as icicles. Their eyes shone.

He gave them all the coins that were in his pockets.

The small boy who had called him 'the funny man that's living in the ruin' said now,

'Thank you, Mr Rolfson.'

And the others chorused, 'A merry Christmas.'

And they went away.

He put on his overcoat – it was a very cold night, with a promise of snow – and walked to Ness. They had a supper of haddock and potatoes and tea. Then they played a few games of draughts and emptied the half-bottle of whisky between them. They had very little left to say to each other, it seemed. 'Come any time,' said Tom Skaill as his visitor left. The first snowflakes were beginning to fall.

His fire was out when he returned to Taing. The house kept a little warmth.

He wrote a letter:

'My dear, I'm writing this on Christmas eve. I hope that you are well and reasonably happy. I think I may have found today what I was looking for here, and I'll be home as soon as the ferry-boat and the plane begin to operate again. Certainly before the end of the year. I am staying in the old Rolfson cottage, alone, happily enough . . .'

Some snow had fallen on the night. When he awoke, he saw through the window part of a great purple-black cloud, freighted with snow. He got up and walked down to the shore. The horizon to the south-east was clear. The sun rose, a point further east than two mornings previously. The sun plucked this morning a brighter string on the great harp of the light.

The White Horse Inn

FISHERMAN

So, Jimmo the fisherman thought, if I get the *Tern* off this reef and the wind doesn't blow the sea up, before the tide turns, I might get to The White Horse for a dram before closing time.

It was a big ebb and the *Tern* was wedged tight in a rock cleft. The wind was rising from the south-west and the waves broke grey and white on the weeded skerries.

'Maybe a farmer will see the trouble I'm in,' said Jimmo.

But the Outertown farmers were busy in the oat harvest.

One girl had wandered from the oatfield down to the seabanks and she stood watching the rock-clenched boat. Jimmo waved and shouted to her, but his voice was lost in the high wind. Her father shouted from the field above. She turned back to the fallen oats and the surging oats and the scythes.

'That was Meg,' said Jimmo. He tried once more to ease the *Tern* off with an oar. The oar slipped in great clusters of wet seaweed.

A wave fell into the boat. The half dozen lobsters stirred themselves.

A light came on in the high farm of Garth.

One by one the harvesters laid down their scythes.

Meg returned to the cliff-edge.

Then Jimmo heard a new sound in the west.

'With all this salt in me,' said Jimmo, 'I could be the eldest son of Lot's wife.'

Then a wave came over the skerry in a wider green swirl. The noises of the tide turning increased in the west, far out, muted, well under the horizon.

A man walked with a lantern from the barn to the byre of Feolquoy.

The girl waved. The fisherman didn't see her. He was intent on the gathering of waters that would be a new wave. The girl's hand drooped. She turned and ran across the meadow.

'I think I'll get to Maggie Marwick's before she closes,' said Jimmo. 'But if I don't sell a lobster or two, will she give me a glass and a pint on tick?'

Three big waves broke from the west over the reef and the *Tern* trembled and reared and was almost free.

HARVESTER

When they drank buttermilk with their cheese and oatcakes in the middle of the morning, and again at three o'clock, he would drink nothing.

Meg and two of the neighbour women came round with the crock of buttermilk and the platter of food.

A few of the men had drunk ale and the rhythm of their reaping was slower than the others.

Mark strode in front, the slow fire smouldering inside him.

The harvesters worked in the field till the last lark was silent and moths were out.

Just after sunset the last of the oatfield was cut.

They all went to the farm for their supper. There was sliced ham and boiled eggs and buttered bannocks on the scrubbed table.

Meg filled the teapot from a big kettle.

'I want nothing to drink,' said Mark.

The lost sun was laving his throat: the jet and scarlet ache of it . . .

The farmer's wife lit a lantern for him and hung it on the outside wall. He splashed water from the pump into his face. His cheeks and his arms were sore.

He walked home over the darkling field.

His mother sat knitting beside the fire, the dog Ben at her feet.

'I'm glad the field's cut,' he said. 'I'm glad our field was cut yesterday. There's coarse weather coming.'

The young man changed into a white shirt without a collar, and put on a cloth cap with the peak behind, and he kicked off his dusty boots and put on shoes with a dull polish on them.

'I warrant,' said the old woman as he left the house, 'you're not going to the gospel meeting.'

'I'm going to the town,' he said, 'to meet the boys.'

'Try and come home decent and respectable,' she said. 'What you need is a good wife. I won't live forever. A good hardworking lass like Meg Richan.'

'Meg Richan has eyes for nobody but Jimmo Smith the fisherman,' said Mark, 'but he doesn't seem to like her all that much. No more do I.'

The rising wind cooled Mark's face as he walked towards Hamnavoe.

The burn that had its source in The Loons mingled sweet dark songs as it flowed under the road and on down to the beach at Warbeth.

Mark paused. He had never heard a more beautiful sound. The harvest sun raged in his throat.

Further up the hill a horse was drinking.

Mark lengthened his stride. He carried his urgent thirst to The White Horse at the north end of Hamnavoe, kept by Mrs Maggie Marwick.

SPINSTER

Miss Mary Ann Thomson emptied the tea-caddy of coppers on to her patterned waxcloth table. They scattered and chimed and lay still. *Well done.* She had exactly, in ha'pennies and farthings and pennies and one threepenny piece, one shilling and sixpence.

She filled the black kettle from the tap and poked the coals in the black stove and set the kettle on top.

She would set out when it was beginning to get dark but before the lamplighter Isaac Flotterston began to draw out his wake of high gas lights along the street. This new amazing thing had been happening for three nights now.

'Tompuss', she said to the grey cat, 'I'm beginning to get a cold, a bad cold. This is the worst time of the year to get a bad cold, in the autumn. Listen, the wind's rising. I'll nip this cold in the bud, Tompuss.'

Simona Flett unlatched the front door and came in. And the words came out of her in a torrent . . . 'Never paid a penny's rent this past year for the shed he's rented from me. One whole pound. Jimmo Smith's father was an honest man all his days and had paid the rent for the shed at Martinmas, always on the very day. And forby William Smith was a sober man. But that weed of a Jimmo put every penny down his throat in drink, either in The Arctic Whaler or The Masons Arms or The White Horse. Advise me, Mary Ann, would I do well to see a lawyer? I think –.'

'I have no time for idle gossip,' said Mary Ann Thomson. 'Jimmo Smith always leaves a haddock at my door. A good-hearted boy, Jimmo. I have a piece of very urgent business along the street. Goodnight.'

Simona Flett eyed the two piles of coins on the sideboard. 'Business. Would that be with Maggie Marwick in The White Horse?' she said, turning up her lip.

'You're an impudent slut,' said Mary Ann Thomson. 'Shut the door after you.'

The whole frame of the door rattled upon Simona Flett's departure.

Mary Ann took a pewter flask from behind the tea caddy on the mantelpiece.

The kettle was beginning to sing on top of the stove.

Tompuss was singing on the rag mat in front of the fire.

'What a person with an oncoming flu does is this,' said Mary Ann Thomson. 'If she has any sense. She pours half the whisky into the big white cup. She puts in three spoons of sugar. She fills to the brim with hot water. She sips slowly in her rocker behind the fire. Then she fills the cup with toddy again and takes it to bed with her and sips and sips. She has a good sleep. In the morning she's cured. She's as right as rain.'

Mary Ann put on her best grey shawl and put the coins in her purse and left the house.

One star was out beside the spire of the Free Kirk.

The sea wind howled up the close and set the shutters rattling in the draper's window. The star seemed to shake in the sky.

On her way to The White Horse, Mary Ann Thomson met only Meg Richan, the farm lass from Outertown. And what would Meg Richan be lingering at the kirk corner for? Some sweetheart or other, most like. The little simpleton that she was.

'What way are you, Mary Ann?' Meg said in a low sweet pure voice.

Mary Ann Thomson, clasping the flask under her shawl, said she had a very bad cold coming on.

'Goodnight, Meg. Go home before the storm blows up.'

MASTER OF THE CHORISTERS

I have observed this burn, Brother Jerome, how in small wise it beginneth, a weeping from a granite rock, grey drops, but in a sudden burst of sun it is tears of joy, silver and blue, a glad clustering.

It loseth itself, in secret laughter, under a weave of heather.

All is lost. The slope flattens, there is a marsh of bog cotton, nor cow can pasture here nor man till. But birds take delight in the shallows.

The thread is not lost. The slow urgent thrust of the stream is there, even among that stagnancy. It spilleth, a shining rill, over a stone lip. There, below, marigolds greet it, and the cress and other simples wherewith Brother Colm, in the good days, used to distil our cures.

It sings. It prates and prattles. There, on a sudden, it is a broad pool, a circle of delight for rowan and blackbird and beard-dripping goat. A herdboy lieth his length to sip the coldness, his throat throbbing. The vain girl kneels and combs out long bright hair (that will be thin grey threads but too soon, and she will take her sere face far from the merciless mirror. All the delightings of men are vanity.)

A waterfall, a *forss*, call and echoing of many trumpets! Let the old prattlers knead their washing here, they cannot hear the parish gossip. I linger often beside the little cataract, and mingle unheard orison with this vibrant outcry of air and water.

Now with a deep grave music it goeth on and down, and through a grassland of sheep and cows and a single galloping white horse, and cometh with joy upon the summer barley fields, that surge a welcome all about the sea-seeking wanderer.

And there, between barleyfield and burn, the mill. A thing of utility for sure, but we see it for what it is, that cunning collocation and ordering of stones and millpond and wheel: man's rapturous response to the positings of earth, wind, water, sun – whereby, at summer's end, the miller hath a granary floor overspilling with golden grains, the superflux of this croft and that, year after year.

Winter cometh soon, when hills are bleak and the burn is frozen. Men do well even in their time of youth, to think of the bitterness of the dark solstice and of death, they must make provision for fire and food, for ale and music, till the first flowers of spring appear, and it is well once more (but fleetingly) with the old man, and a wonderment, all, to the new child.

Beyond those shadows, images, symbols, Brother Jerome, is this abiding truth that we solemnly and with eager questing seek all our days: uttering it forth in psalms day after day, eight-fold. *Panis angelicus.*

I greet you well from Orkney.

The burn endeth in the ocean, below our little monastery.

The bishop, as you know, gave the brothers leave to live out the rest of their time in the monastery. I am the last brother left. No farm boys bring pure voices now to my song-school, this long while. A slow dilapidation undoes arch and apse. I lack strength now to gather and set new stone.

May this letter reach you at last, in Ireland.

One of the earl's men, William Clark, is building him a

tavern at the end of the bay three miles from here. They will call it, I hear, The White Horse. He has a well-handed wife called Mareon that will bake and brew for seafarers and horsemen.

LAMPLIGHTER

Splash! The first gas lamp exploded soundlessly into light an hour after sunset.

A troop of children cheered.

The lamplighter strode on, with his two long poles, one flame-tipped.

The children followed.

The gas light at the corner of the Town Hall, high, illumined the Old Orkney distillery and the front of Billy Clouston's pub.

Splash, and Alfred Square was an island of light.

People came to their doors to watch the lighting of the new street lamps.

Isaac Flotterston shouldered his long poles and strode on.

Children came dancing after. There were three more children now.

A huge boy-child, Tommy Ronaldson, a mongol, gaped with delight. He followed, first, the magician.

The lamplighter carried, carefully folded, a letter in his pocket. ('We, the baillies and councillors of the burgh of Hamnavoe, appoint you Isaac Flotterston, to be lamplighter in the burgh, at a fee of ten pounds a year on top of your wages as dustman, to illuminate the new gas lamps along the street of the said burgh one hour after sunset, and afterwards at midnight to extinguish the said lamps. On the three nights round about the time of the full moon, it will not be necessary to ignite the lamps. It is further laid down that the lamplighter shall abstain from imbibing of intoxicating waters during his hours of duty . . .')

One pole, questing high, turned the gas tap in the lamp. One, flame-tipped, set the gas hissing and exploding silently into yellow light in its high glass tower.

The wind flung the lamplight about the Post Office, the Library, and Melvin Place.

Mark Ritch the ploughboy came down the steep road and hesitated at the wavering edge of the street light.

The lamplighter strode on. Over Flett's Inn, on the steep down-slope of the street, he angled one pole, then the other. *Splash!* Dundas Street was douched in brightness. Three drinking men came to the door of Flett's. 'A drink for thee, Isaac, inside' . . .

Isaac never so much as glanced at them.

Into the windy darkness ahead he strode.

The big mongol boy and the children followed.

The Plainstones, the United Presbyterian Church, the Bank. *Splash!* – the lamp over the watchmaker's exploded and flung brightness about those places that had never known such light before.

Up one narrow close from the pier below came Jimmo Smith, fisherman. He carried a box containing six blue slithering scrithing lobsters.

Isaac, light-bearer, strode past The Masons Arms. A melodeon was playing inside. Two uncertain voices sang. 'No singing,' shouted the landlord.

Splash! The gas light at the corner of 'The Masons Arms', high up, scattered waverings of light into twenty nooks and corners.

The landlord, light-besplendoured, stood in the open door. 'A dram for you, Isaac, to celebrate a new milestone in the march of progress.'

'Tomorrow,' said Isaac solemnly, 'at street sweeping time.'

He led his troop of children, laughers and dancers, into boreal darkness.

Once he glanced behind. The stars were washed from the sky.

At the Pier-head, above the circular horse-trough called The Fountain, in memory of Hamnavoe's hero and municipal martyr, Alexander Graham, a gas lamp had been set. Isaac Flotterston applied his two wands, one after the other. *Splash!* The five louts and hangers-on and penniless cadgers for drink were startled into light and looking and a passing unease.

Miss Mary Ann Thomson retreated from the soundless explosion of light. Then she walked round the edge of the windy circle, one fist tight about the heavy pewter flask inside her shawl.

'Dram night, Mary Ann,' said a useless drouth from the harbourmaster's door-step. 'Put a good swash of water in it.' The Pier-head loungers laughed.

Miss Thomson walked along the river of light that was now the street to her house. Her face was set like a stone.

Isaac Flotterston, going the other way, under the ancient stars, stopped.

'Here,' said Isaac to the big mongol boy. 'You can carry one pole for me' . . . Tommy Ronaldson's face became a round of purest joy. His almond eyes were slits of delight. He shouldered the pole as a soldier sets his pike.

Isaac strode gravely under the stars that were soon, over Hamnavoe, to be cinders forever.

Tommy followed. The numerous children danced behind.

Splash! And the new lamp at the corner of the Temperance Hotel hissed and spluttered and sang brightness. Gas-light segments crashed silently into Lieutenant Miller's close with its heraldic lintel and broke against the Royal Mail steamer *St Ola* at her berth and the Grimsby trawler at the pier, sheltering. The harbour waves, a light upon them never before known, snarled against the wooden jetty.

'It is well done,' said Isaac Flotterston.

Isaac felt tired. The feeling of being a magician was ebbing out of him. 'Follow,' he said to Tommy who carried the pole for turning on the gas tap. 'There's only two more lamps.'

At the next lamp, beside the coach station where the horses were stabled, there was disaster!

The lamplighter took the first pole from Tommy and turned on the gas. He thrust up the flame-tipped pole. The gas mantle shivered into a hundred white light flakes. The naked gas flame roared in the high wind.

'It is possible,' said Isaac solemnly, 'that there will be a new lamplighter in Hamnavoe as from tomorrow.'

They went forward, more slowly, a dispirited company.

Two large tears coursed down Tommy Ronaldson's face.

'There's only one more lamp,' said Isaac Flotterston. 'I will finish my work. Tomorrow is a new day. There's nothing to girn about. Follow.'

The last lamp was set high on the corner of The White Horse inn. Very cautiously Isaac applied both his magic poles, one after the other. The White Horse and the blacksmith's yard opposite and the road to the Market Green beyond were glorified with splashings of the new promethean fire.

The children clapped their hands.

Tommy, his bulging face tear-stained still, held his pole gladly.

'Tommy,' said the lamplighter. 'Hold this other pole for a minute or two. There's a good boy. I must go into The White Horse and see Mistress Marwick about some business.'

Isaac Flotterston went into The White Horse with its one wretched paraffin lamp hanging beside the gantry.

SCHOOLMASTER

'Be clear about this,' said Mr Reith the headmaster, 'I have no objection to a man taking a drink within reason.'

'I understand that,' said Mr Hodgkiss, who had been appointed to teach English, History, Religious subjects, and junior Latin at the start of the summer term. 'That's good,' he said.

'But one must conform to the mores of the populace – I mean, those of them who count,' said Mr Reith.

'I am here, in this school,' said Mr Hodgkiss, 'to share with such of my pupils who can rise to it, the joy and wisdom of man's accumulated experience over the centuries.'

'You put it very well,' said Mr Reith.

'It sounds pompous,' said Mr Hodgkiss, 'put that way. Forgive me. What I mean is, wine and wisdom and beauty have always gone together.'

'Maybe so,' said Mr Reith. 'I must tell you now, frankly, there are complaints. Parents, members of the school board, the kirk session. There have been anonymous letters.'

'About what?' said Mr Hodgkiss.

'That you go openly and unashamedly into public houses. The thing is – what they think is – what they hold as an unshakeable tenet is, that school teachers should show an example to the whole community.'

'What kind of example?'

'Of temperance.'

'Sir, Mr Reith, I am the personification of temperance. Temperance and total abstinence are different things entirely. Nobody has seen me being wheeled home drunk from

The Arctic Whaler or The White Horse. Nor will they. I go there to enjoy the company of my fellow-townsmen, the street sweepers and the fishermen and the sailors. I enjoy their company better than the company of councillors, bank clerks, shopkeepers, justices-of-the-peace, those anyway I have met so far in this town. I will continue as I have begun.'

'Dick,' said Mr Reith, 'if I may call you that in friendship and in fellowship – I enjoy a drink, nobody more. But I drink in the privacy of my own fireside, without offence to anyone. Or I drink in the company of my social equals. I have been fifteen years headmaster in this school. No one has pointed a finger.'

'Well, sir,' said Mr Hodgkiss, 'I thank you for your advice. I will think about it.'

'Please do,' said Mr Reith. 'Think very seriously about it.'

In Mrs Scad's lodging house in Franklin Road, Richard Hodgkiss, Master of Arts of Edinburgh University, took off his collar and tie in his bed-sitting room. Seeing that it was a windy autumn night with an arctic edge to it, he put on a thick pullover.

Mrs Scad was standing in the lobby, in the light from her kitchen.

'You'll be going out to see the street lamps. Isn't that one in Graham Place just beautiful?' said Mrs Scad.

'I like the starlight better,' said Mr Hodgkiss.

'Wrap up well,' said Mrs Scad. 'I would put on that thick woollen scarf.'

'I'm keeping that scarf for the snow,' said Mr Hodgkiss.

'Will you be wanting cocoa tonight?'

'Not tonight, Mrs Scad, thank you.'

Under some of the gas lights a few townsfolk were standing. The wind whipped the men's coats about their knees. One or two drifted from lamp to lamp, entranced.

Mr Hodgkiss greeted the light-splashed townsmen. Only one or two raised an uncertain hand. None spoke.

He noticed that one of the street lamps had no mantle. The naked flame snored and flapped in the gale.

Mr Hodgkiss, approaching the last lamp at the corner of The White Horse, saw Captain McCallum, retired shipmaster and chairman of the School Board, walking rapidly from the gate of his big house towards the illumined street. His dog trotted behind him. He smote the ground with his stick, a brisk nautical rhythm.

'Hodgkiss, is it? Evening, Hodgkiss. Admiring the gas lamps, are you? The best thing to come to Hamnavoe in my time. Don't you agree?'

'No,' said Mr Hodgkiss.

'You'll get used to it. We'll see the full benefit in the depth of winter. Enjoy your walk, Hodgkiss.'

'I'm only walking as far as The White Horse for a drink.'

Captain McCallum looked at Mr Hodgkiss, stern-faced. The schoolmaster could smell wafts of whisky from the old skipper's breath. 'I would go very carefully if I were you, Hodgkiss. Very very carefully indeed.'

Captain McCallum smote the flagstone so violently with his brass-tipped walking stick that three sparks spurted and died.

'Goodnight, captain,' said Mr Hodgkiss cheerfully. The captain strode on very rapidly towards the bright pools of light along the street. Here and there a townsman lifted his hat to Captain McCallum.

Mr Hodgkiss laughed.

He turned to the door of The White Horse.

There, under the last street lamp, a country girl was standing. Her head was bowed so that Mr Hodgkiss could not see her face.

'Are you waiting for somebody?' said Mr Hodgkiss.

The girl raised her head. Mr Hodgkiss saw that she had been crying. A bright tear ran down her cheek. A gust scattered the bead of grief from the girl and Mr Hodgkiss felt, at the corner of his mouth, a small saltness.

Inside The White Horse someone laughed.

INNKEEPER

After the last customer had gone at eleven o'clock and she had washed and wiped the glasses and the counter and put the gantry to rights, Mrs Maggie Marwick, proprietrix of The White Horse inn, wrote a letter to her sister in Canada on sheets of lined account paper.

'Dear Harriet, Once more I take pen in hand to write to you. Things have been quiet here ever since the herring season stopped. Tonight is the quietest night for a long time, I think everybody is so taken with the new street lamps. I wouldn't be surprised if there wasn't some terrible accident with that gas, an explosion and lives lost. The Council talked me into putting a lamp at the corner of the inn. I wish now I had given them a hard *No*.

'As I say it has been a quiet night for business with only a few patrons. Mary Ann Thomson, I have to laugh when I think of her and the cold she gets on her chest every fortnight regular, she came with her quarter flask and forced a cough or two out of her and off with her then with the full flask under her shawl. Then there was that nice boy Mark Ritch the farm servant at Breckness, I never saw anybody drinking 4 scooners of Flett's ale so fast. Well I can't blame him it's hot work in the harvest, as we both know well. Poor Jimmo Smith of course had no money but I gave him a big glass of Old Orkney and a scooner for the six lobsters he had in his fishbox and he sat quite happy at the fire, I think he was cold after being out west all day. Jimmo and Mark get on together fine, not like some of them weekend brawlers I have to throw out by the scruff of their necks. Pat came in the Irish tinker, and drank his scooner and went away again without offence. Some Hamnavoe publicans won't let Pat over their doorstep.

'That Isaac Flotterston the rubbish collector was here, he does most of his drinking in the Masons Arms. Would you believe it, they've given him the lamplighter's job, they must be out of their minds. I suppose The White Horse lamp being the last lamp he dropped in by to celebrate. Well he was half-seas-across when he left at eleven, the poor creature he must have forgot he must put the lamps out again at midnight. Ah well.

'That new school teacher was here again, a nice good-looking young man, Mr Hodgkiss. Call me Dick, says he. But nobody does, I for one know my place. He wants to be friendly, he tried to get into talk with Mark and Jimmo over by the fire, but they just mumbled into their beer mugs and looked away. I don't know what to think about him, the children like him very much, so does his landlady, Janet Scad, but I hear the authorities are worried about him mixing too freely with every Tom Dick and Harry and never darkening the door of a kirk. Anyway Isaac the rubbish man scrounged a drink off him and then Mr Hodgkiss quizzed me about some lass or other that was crying in the street. What would I know about that? He never seemed to see the tinker at all.

'Well, Harriet, I think it will be quiet in The White Horse from now till the Lammas Fair in September. The froth will fly that day, the drouths will jostle in The White Horse like herring in a net . . .'

The Tree and the Harp

So, the dreadful old woman was dead at last. Old rich Mrs Maida was lying still and cold in her bed in the big house called the Hall.

The Hall stood down at the shore, an eighteenth-century house with a large garden surrounded by a high wall, so that Mrs Maida might have privacy from the coarse islanders.

One or two islanders there had to be inside the precincts, the two gardeners, (one of whom, Sam, looked after the hives and the honey) and Miss Troll, the housekeeper who lived in the lodge – she had learned her trade in rich important houses in the south, and was even snootier than old Mrs Maida, though more prim – and Mrs Birsay the cook and cleaner, and Mrs Birsay's girl Sophie, aged twelve. (Mrs Birsay was a widow.)

Sophie was glad that Mrs Maida was dead. She didn't exactly sing and dance; but she felt a shadow lift from her. That terrible voice, that sarcasm that was like the flash and bite of a sword, would frighten Sophie no more!

At breakfast-time her mother had come downstairs and whispered in the kitchen, 'She's dead! Poor Mrs Maida died in the night . . .' And then touched her eyes with the corner of her apron; for Mrs Birsay was a gentle-hearted woman. She had suffered greatly under Mrs Maida – no tyrant could have afflicted a loyal subject so horribly.

And Sophie wept to see her mother weeping. But inside, her heart was like a bird.

Only two weeks since that black voice had been ringing through the big house. 'Woman, this steak pie isn't fit to eat!' . . . 'You, woman, what d'you call yourself, Mrs Birsay, I nearly broke my teeth on the buns you baked this morning' . . . 'Birsay, you slut, there's a cobweb on the painting of my grandfather the general – there, woman, at the corner of the frame – clean it at once!' . . . 'No, I do *not* want a cup of tea. Say tea to me once more and I'll strangle you.'

And Sophie's mother had taken all these lies and insults and said nothing.

She knew her place, Sophie's mother.

Besides, if Mrs Maida had dismissed her, which she might well have done in one of her terrible tantrums, where could mother and daughter have gone?

There was no place in the world for them. Nowhere.

Sophie's father had been a sailor. They had lived in a rented house in the village. One winter, when Sophie was ten, a telegram had come – Bill Birsay had been lost at sea, swept overboard in a gale in Biscay.

They had had to be out of the house by November. After the grief, that was a gnawing worry. They had no relatives in the island. They were alone, and poor.

For many nights that summer Mrs Birsay and Sophie sat silent, looking into the fire, the tea growing cold in their cups.

Occasionally a man with a brief-case from the National Assistance office would come and ask tart questions.

One night there had come a prim knock on the cottage door. It was prim Miss Troll from the big house. 'It has come to Mrs Maida's notice that you might be available for general duties up at the Hall. Cooking and cleaning. Mrs Maida is very particular. She has a delicate stomach. She cannot bear untidiness in any shape or form. Please come to be interviewed at the Hall by Mrs Maida tomorrow morning at 10 A.M. Should you prove acceptable, a room will be provided for you and the girl.'

And Mrs Birsay had gone to be interviewed – a harrowing experience – and she had been accepted. She was to start on Monday morning. Ten pounds a week, room and fire and food free; Wednesday afternoons off.

Mrs Birsay could have hugged Mrs Maida with gratitude. But one look from that basilisk eye quelled her.

'Thank you, ma'am,' murmured Mrs Birsay, and curtsied.

And so mother and daughter moved into the big house, at the beginning of spring.

And really, it was a nice little room on the ground floor they had, with a rosebush outside the window, and blackbirds singing from morning to night, and pigeons hopping and cooing round the kitchen door.

The garden was lovely. A little burn crept through it and out into the sea beyond the high wall. The burn, unfortunately, was sluggish and weed-choked and muted. Under the single tree it broadened into a dark deep pool, that looked sinister in the sunlight.

It would have been heaven for Sophie, if it hadn't been for the tyrant on the floor above. 'Listen, Mrs Birsay or whatever you call yourself, I can't eat soup with carrots or peas or onions in it. Please remember that!' . . . 'Woman, I didn't sleep a wink last night – you made the bed up all wrong' . . . 'Mrs Birsay, I don't want that girl of yours – what's her name, Sophie – wandering all over the garden. She'll ruin the flower-beds. *There's to be no climbing up that sycamore tree beside the pool* – I will *not* have your girl doing that' . . . 'Woman, come here at once – drop everything, a button has come off my blouse, sew it on' . . . 'How many times do I have to tell you, I only drink tea with my breakfast' . . . 'Do you ever think of anything but tea?'

So began this hideous tyranny that lasted for six months.

It had to be put up with. There was nothing else for it. Apart from the ten pounds a week, they were slaves.

How Sophie would have loved to wander through the forbidden garden! But if she set foot beyond the pavement that girdled the house one or other of the gardeners was there to shoo her away. They had been given their orders.

Even after the gardeners went home, at sunset, it was impossible. Mrs Maida was always on the watch from her high window, like a hawk.

But one night of full moon Sophie did it! Her mother was busy in the kitchen, preparing tomorrow's dinner. Miss Troll had gone to a church meeting. The tyrant had been in bed all day with a headache; her curtains were drawn.

Sophie looked: the curtains were still drawn. The moon had risen clear of the high garden wall. Beads of dew flashed from the flower-beds near and far, in the light of the full moon. And now the moon was looking through the sycamore leaves into the pool.

It was pure enchantment.

It was more than Sophie could bear.

She went like a shadow across the lawn. She stood under the tree. She seized the lowest branch and swung herself up into the tree. And the leaves whispered all about her.

Sophie looked down into the pool. It was dark and stagnant and sinister.

Then she heard a voice. 'Hello, I wish I had known you. Thirty years ago – thirty Julys – I sat in that tree. You're the first girl to sit in that fork of the tree since that night thirty years ago. Welcome.'

Sophie was so startled she almost fell out of the tree. The voice had been sweet, distinct, beautiful.

Yet it was difficult to locate the music of the voice, precisely. There was certainly no one to be seen, neither in the tree nor at the pool's edge nor among the bushes and flower-beds.

Sophie was on the point of dismissing the words as a part of the night's enchantment (for everything was lovely beyond words, really, and made perilous by the deep dark flashing pool below, and by the possibility that a dreadful eye was looking at her from the edge of a curtain.) Oh, she had never felt so moved and excited! She would tell nobody, not even her mother.

Now she *must* go in. She would be missed.

'I was a girl once, too.'

There was no mistaking the voice this time.

There was sadness in it, and loss, and pleading.

Sophie looked everywhere.

There was no girl to be seen.

The moon went behind a cloud.

Sophie dropped out of the tree. She moved across the garden like a shadow.

'Where have you been, Sophie? You look as if you'd seen a ghost. I'll put on the kettle for tea. Have you done your lessons? Oh, dear, I hope Mrs Maida will like this roast chicken, cold! I know it'll be good' . . .

Mrs Maida did not like the roast chicken. For five days she liked nothing that was offered to her.

She lay in bed, sipping barley water, with the blinds drawn, growling and complaining.

'Something, woman – surely there's *something* you can cook that'll lie on my stomach . . . That custard was like yellow peril – take it away . . . Can't you even poach an egg properly? – I've had heartburn all day after that egg . . . No, I do *not* want a nice cup of tea! . . .'

If it wasn't food, it was something else. 'This pillow's as hard as a stone' . . . 'I said I wanted a hot-water bottle, not a wishy-washy lukewarm thing' . . . 'That girl of yours, Sophie, makes far too much noise in the morning going to school – clack clack clack over the paving – can't you get her a pair of soft shoes?' . . .

No doubt about it, the tyranny in the big house was growing blacker and heavier.

Even Miss Troll felt the lash of that tongue, and would pass up and down stairs with thin grey lips.

As for Mrs Birsay, nothing she did was right.

Sophie knew that her mother was the very best cook and housekeeper in the island.

It was shameful, the way she was treated.

One had to make allowances for an invalid. But it was very difficult.

Now old Mrs Maida was more often in bed than out of it.

Dr MacIntyre called every day. Not even he was spared. 'Are you sure you're a proper doctor and not a quack? That last bottle you gave me nearly killed me. I want another prescription this time – something quite different. I sometimes think I'd be better with a tinker wife and her herbs' . . .

If, once or twice, Sophie came face to face with the dreadful old woman in the long corridor, she turned and fled! 'That's right, you little brat, off with you, get your mother to poison you with that awful tea she's forever making' . . .

But those chance encounters became fewer and fewer.

The old tyrant was getting weaker, no doubt about it.

Now, in late summer, she only got out of bed to shuffle on Miss Troll's arm to the garden chair between the rose bush and the fuchsia bush.

'Not there, you fool!' she wheezed one day when Miss Troll had set the garden chair for her under the sycamore tree, beside the pool. 'You ought to know better! Over there, beside the red roses . . .'

But, after five or ten minutes, it was, 'The bees are bothering me . . . There, I've got hayfever again – it's that farmer cutting his hay. I could wring the fool's neck . . . Take me inside.'

Illness had made her more dreadful, in Sophie's eyes. She glared here and there out of her grey shrunken mask of a face.

And Miss Troll had to summon Mrs Birsay to help carry the old rich wreck of a woman up to her bed.

Only twice in the month of August did Mrs Maida venture into the beautiful garden – and then only briefly. The butterflies revelled silently about her departure, as she hobbled in on Miss Troll's arm.

And the two gardeners would light their pipes and have a rest. It was a large house of twenty rooms. For Sophie, it was forbidden territory; she was confined to the bed-sitting room and the kitchen.

'Oh,' her mother would cry, 'it's such a sad house! All the rooms blinded, all the lovely furniture covered in sheets. The loveliest room of all is the music room. O Sophie, how I wish I could take you to the music room! But I can't. Mrs Maida has forbidden it, strictly.'

(Mrs Birsay had to dust the deserted part of the house twice a week.)

Sophie's curiosity, as harvest-time came and the farm-folk cut their barley in the fields around, narrowed to the music room. Sophie loved music, but – other than sing – she had no chance to do anything about it. To play the piano well was her greatest ambition. But that was out of the question; there was no piano available, and furthermore her mother couldn't afford to send her to the lady in the village who gave piano tuition.

As the darker nights of autumn drew in, Mrs Birsay spent most of her time sewing and knitting. Now the mistress of the big house could take only the lightest of food: fruit juices, poached fish, beaten-up eggs. So Mrs Birsay justified her existence by knitting bed socks for the invalid, and making curtains of the old rich materials she had found in a chest in the attic; so that it might cheer up the invalid.

But all she did was grumble. Nothing was right. Her voice had lost its black edge. It was old and grey and hopeless now.

'What do I want fine curtains for? They should have been hung thirty years ago . . . what did you say the name of your girl was? Sophie? Tell Sophie she can sing if she wants to – she has a nice voice. I heard her the other evening, singing under my window . . . No tea, not even for breakfast – it tastes of nothing . . . Nothing tastes of anything any more . . . I feel very tired . . . Tell that Troll woman not to come near me. She looks more and more like an undertaker or a gravedigger . . . The curtains are quite pretty, Mrs Birsay, but they're thirty years too late – Tell Sophie she is *not to go into the garden* . . .'

It was pathetic, Mrs Birsay told Sophie, to see how weak and shrunken the old lady had become.

'I think,' said Mrs Birsay, 'she'll never be out of that bed again . . .'

Why did those words put a sudden glitter in Sophie's eyes?

The big house was quiet after tea.

Miss Troll had gone to visit another spinster who lived at the far end of the island, on WRI business.

Mrs Birsay was sewing cushion covers out of the roll of material she had uncovered in the attic. The mistress had said she could do anything she liked with it. Mrs Maida, once her health began to improve, might enjoy bright cushions in the rooms, instead of the old sun-faded ones. So Mrs Birsay sewed and hemmed and drank endless cups of tea.

The old invalid was presumably drowsing in her bed. More and more she was lost under the tides of sleep.

Sophie, without a word, slipped out of the room, and began to explore the house. She carried a candle with a yellow flower of flame floating above.

Where was the music room?

Oh, it was eerie! Sophie opened room after room – each, in the candle-light, was an immense silent theatre of shadows. The shadows crowded about her. All the chairs and tables covered, as if they were dead and waiting for the worms. Sophie shut door after door. Her thudding heart must be the loudest thing in the house.

Once a drop of hot candle wax fell on her hand! She almost screamed.

She opened a door. Another dance of shadows, a silent gathering. Ah, but this must be the music room. That shrouded shape over there could only be the piano! Sophie moved over towards the piano. Her glimmer of light discovered a white bust on the mantelshelf, with the name 'Chopin' on the base – and over there, against the wall, a Celtic harp. Sophie touched a string – it gave out a rich pure note – the whole house seemed to echo the golden sound.

A voice said, 'Oh, if I had known you thirty years ago! . . . We would have had such happy times . . . Yes, I'd have taught you to play the harp, and the piano too . . . I think I'd have had no better friend than you . . . Too late, too late . . .'

The voice was clear and unmistakable; it was the voice she had heard in the garden.

This time, there was no enchantment of moonlight to shake it out of the nothingness; only a feeble candle-flame, and a harp stroke.

Sophie was not in the least afraid: there was such an air of welcome in the music room, though it was tinged by sadness and regret, a little.

The reverberations of the harp stroke seemed to go on for a long time. Then the room was stark and cold again.

Sophie stayed there as long as she dared.

She *must* go back – she would be missed. (She ought to have been bent over her home-work.)

She descended the wide stair, softly, led by the yellow petal of flame.

Coming round the corner into the long corridor that ended in the kitchen, Sophie almost ran into a frail figure lingering at the foot of the great stairway.

The girl cried out with terror! It was Mrs Maida. The candle fell on the floor and went out.

The old woman put leaf-light hands on Sophie's shoulder. 'Sunniva, I heard you at the harp, dear,' she said. 'It was lovely. I thought there would never be music in this house, ever again . . . Oh, I know it's lonely for you here in this big house, I know it is. I can't think what to do about that, Sunniva. You can't mix with the village girls. That's out of the question. I know you'd like to speak to them, maybe invite a girl or two up to the house. I'll think about it. Maybe some day. It's hard to know what to do for the best . . . If only your parents were still alive . . . Yes, dear, you can walk in the garden if you like. It's such a lovely night. Then supper and bed. What, you'd like to climb up into that tree? I don't see why not. You're light and strong enough . . .'

What was the old woman talking about?

'I'm Sophie,' said the girl. 'I'm sorry for wandering about the house like this. I didn't do any harm.'

'Come and kiss me goodnight once you're in from the garden, Sunniva,' said Mrs Maida in a gentle voice.

Then she put her twisted hand on the bannister and began slowly to climb the stair to her room.

That night, she died.

Miss Troll came into her own, briefly, making arrangements for the funeral. Only the gentry were invited, of course, and the village merchant and the farmer from the big farm and the local councillor and Dr MacIntyre. As things turned out, very few attended the funeral in the little family burial-place next to the Hall. The weather was bad. And nobody liked the dead woman very much.

Miss Troll had done the things that ought to be done at a funeral. There was sherry for the mourners, and plates of smoked salmon on toast, and little cakes that Mrs Birsay had made. The few mourners lingered awhile in the drawing room, made a few valedictory remarks, then went away with their long insincere faces.

Miss Troll permitted herself a thin smile as the last of them went. She had done her duty.

Neither Mrs Birsay nor Sophie had been invited to the funeral, of course.

Mrs Birsay had the longest face of all, not only that day but for several days to come. From time to time she touched her eyes with the corner of her apron. The kettle was always on the boil. The teapot was never empty.

What would become of her and Sophie now? Once more they would be out in the cold winds . . .

'You may stay where you are meantime,' said Miss Troll. 'Mrs Maida was the last of the family. No doubt the house will be sold. The family lawyers in Edinburgh have the disposing of the estate. We will just carry on as we're doing until we receive official notice . . . No doubt my services to Mrs Maida, extending over forty years, will not be forgotten' . . .

This last sentence was spoken with a tinge of anxiety. It was obvious that Miss Troll was not at all sure as to how things would fall out. If she had been, she would not have spoken the way she did to a mere servant like Mrs Birsay. It was the first time Miss Troll had ever visited the Birsays' room.

As the days passed, anxiety began to eat into her more and more. She took to visiting Mrs Birsay twice or thrice a day in the kitchen. (Mrs Birsay was a good listener.) She even condescended to drink cups of tea.

'I was very faithful to Mrs Maida,' she said; permitting Sophie's mother to pour her yet another cup of tea. 'I might go so far as to say, I sacrificed my prospects for her. For, after the terrible thing happened, she was almost out of her mind. Had I not been there to support her who knows what she might not have done? I was a rock of strength to her, when she needed me most. And I devoted all the rest of my days to her. I'm sure she won't have forgotten me in her will. But did she ever *make* a will? She didn't like talk of death and wills and tombstones – she couldn't stand the thought of her latter end. The lawyers in Edinburgh, they must know what I've sacrificed for Mrs Maida . . .'

So that was it – the prim proud spinster was even more terrified than Mrs Birsay as to what might become of her, now that the earth had closed over the mistress of the house.

She had lived for forty years in the lodge at the end of the drive: it was a part of her; it was unthinkable that ever she might have to leave it.

'There are no immediate relatives,' said Miss Troll. 'There are, I think, some distant cousins in Canada and South Africa. They were little help to her when the tragedy happened. They never even wrote a letter of sympathy. In fact, I doubt if Mrs Maida had even *seen* them all her life long. How awful, if they were to inherit the estate!'

'Well,' said Mrs Birsay, 'it must have been a sad thing for her indeed, losing her husband.'

'Pooh!' said Miss Troll. 'She never shed a tear for *him*. Mr Maida had his own house, in Perthshire. I quite liked Mr Maida, he was always civil to me. Then suddenly he left, without so much as a goodbye. Mind you, Mrs Maida could sometimes be a difficult person to live with. Between you and me, but for Charles, their son, he'd have left her much sooner. As soon as Charles was found a suitable position in the city, and settled, Mr Maida was up and off . . .

'A son!' cried Mrs Birsay. 'So there's a son!'

'There *was* a son,' said Miss Troll. 'He was killed in a car crash in Yorkshire, himself and his wife, two years after they were married. They were on their way north, for a holiday, with the baby, to see her.'

'That was a terrible thing to happen!' said Mrs Birsay. 'No wonder she had her dark moods from time to time.'

'She didn't roll a tear down her cheek for that either,' said Miss Troll. 'Not one single tear, that ever I saw. She was like one of those ancient Roman matrons you read about – all strength and resolution.'

'And the baby, it was killed too?' sighed Mrs Birsay.

'Oh, no. The child survived . . . "What home or institution will I place the creature in?" Mrs Maida said twenty times if she said it once in the course of the next few days, while the funeral arrangements were going on. (Mr and Mrs Charles are buried out there too, in the same place as the mistress.) "I can't have a brat about here," she declared. "I couldn't put up with it for an hour" . . . Then suddenly, on the evening of the double funeral, she rounded on me and she declared, "Troll, I think I'd better have this grandchild here. I'll give it a try, anyway" . . .'

'The poor child!' said Mrs Birsay – and at once she could have bit out her tongue for saying it.

'Not poor child in the slightest,' said Miss Troll. 'I never in my life beheld such a beautiful happy child, right from the start. And that same child caused a miracle in this house. The stream ran, the desert blossomed as a rose. That same child, I assure you, gave Mrs Maida twelve years of the most wonderful happiness! It was a blessing in her life. This house seemed to be overflowing with music and laughter all the time . . . Ah, she played the piano like an angel, Sunniva. Alas!'

'What happened?' whispered Mrs Birsay, and brought the corner of her apron up to her eyes again.

'You see that tree out there in the garden?' said Miss Troll. 'Over there by the pool. One summer evening Sunniva – that was her name – climbed up into the tree. A branch broke. She fell into the pool and was drowned. Nobody saw it. The gardeners lifted her body out of the pool next morning, and carried it into the house. "Lay her in the music room," said Mrs Maida coldly . . .'

Mrs Birsay choked on her sobs; beyond speech she was.

'From that day,' said Miss Troll, 'winter and night descended on this house. I thought, for a month and more afterwards, that she would go mad. Dr MacIntyre shook his head. "It's more than you or I can handle, Miss Troll," he said. "If she could weep," he said, "she might improve. As things are, she'll will herself into the grave. What's the name of that old Greek sculptor whose statues seemed to have the breath of life in them? – here we have the opposite process, a living woman turning herself to stone in front of our eyes. I can't do a thing about it" . . . For a month she did not speak. She hardly moved. I think, though, she cried in secret. I would see her, morning after morning, with the stains on her face. Then one morning she spoke. "Troll," she said, "I want all the rooms closed up. Cover the furniture. Draw the blinds. Stop the clocks. Only the few needful rooms are to be used" . . . So, in a way, she recovered. But the terrible scar was in her mind and heart and spirit to her dying day . . . Not that she ever mentioned Sunniva. One day, some time later, I happened to say, "That sycamore, it might be better cut down, don't you think? And the pool is stagnant – it ought to be drained?" . . . Oh, Mrs Birsay, I have never before or since endured such a storm of rage! The tree and the pool would stand till they rotted! I was never to mention such a thing again . . . Poor silly me, I never know when enough is enough – I suppose it might have been a year later that I said, "Mrs Maida, the girl Seenie", (Seenie used to come twice a week to dust and polish) – "Seenie," I said, "tells me one of the harp-strings is broken in the music room. Will I have it seen to?" Such a sudden blaze of anger! "Nobody is to touch a thing in the music room, now or at any other time. Never so much as mention music room again, you withered old witch!" . . . So, Mrs Birsay, I learned my lesson the hard way. Many a time I was sore tempted to leave her. But time passed, and I grew older, and at last I knew I would stay with her till the end.'

'I have never heard anything so sad!' sighed Mrs Birsay. 'Poor Mrs Maida – I forgive her the one or two hard things she said to me.'

'It's come at last,' said Miss Troll, producing a letter from her handbag. 'A solicitor from the firm in Edinburgh is coming on Monday. For some reason, he wants to see you and Sophie also. I suppose it's a good sign that the letter's addressed to me . . . No, thank you, Mrs Birsay, I won't have any more tea.'

Miss Troll's hand trembled as she put the letter back into her handbag.

Sophie raced through the big house, room after room, pulling up blinds, tearing the covers from chairs, tables, sideboards, throwing open the windows so that, after thirty years' stagnation, the air could flow in.

She was behaving like a crazy girl.

Sometimes she laughed. Sometimes she cried. She had to sit down, from time to time, for a little rest. But never for long. It was out into the corridor with her, into another room: the blinds jerked up, window sash opened, covers whisked off. Beautiful hidden objects declared themselves: clocks, bookcases, bowls and jars of great beauty, tapestried chairs, portraits in gilt frames, round oak tables.

And they were all hers!

Sophie threw open a high drawing-room window. The two gardeners, Sam and Willie, were idling below – since Mrs Maida's death they had turned noticeably lazier. 'Hey, you two!' shouted Sophie. 'I want that pool under the tree cleaned out at once. Do you hear me? I want the burn to go singing into it and out the other side, like it used to do. Get started!'

Sam and Willie turned astonished faces up at her.

'Your wages are to be increased by five pounds a week,' cried Sophie.

Then she ran along the corridor to another room that had been in silent mourning for thirty years, and let the air and the light in, and set free the lovely furniture, pictures, ornaments. She adjusted the weights in the tall bronze clock. The pendulum swung – time began again in the room.

She had to sit down and have a longer rest. The wonder of all that had happened that day had exhausted her.

An hour ago the Edinburgh lawyer had left the house, having read the will.

It was the strangest will ever read.

The memory of Miss Troll's face, at the part that concerned her, sent Sophie into another wild outburst of merriment . . . 'To Martha Troll, my companion, I leave and bequeath one pot of honey a month, in the vain hope that it may sweeten her disposition' . . .

Sophie had never seen anything so droll as the look on Miss Troll's face then! The girl rocked back and fore in the chair with laughter. She laughed till tears streamed down her cheeks.

Delight and wonderment echoed in room after room. It was hers – all hers!

The look on her mother's face had been almost as comical. 'To my cook and cleaning-woman, Mrs Sandra Birsay, as her existence seems to be devoted to the brewing of tea, I leave my best china teapot, along with half-a-dozen matching cups and saucers, so that she can make tea everlasting from this day to the day of her funeral' . . .

'That lovely teapot mine!' Mrs Birsay had cried. 'How kind!'

As for Miss Troll, after the first horrified gape at the lawyer's mouth pronouncing sentence, an extraordinary sequence of expressions had passed across her face: bewilderment, disbelief, self-pity, sorrow, rage, resignation, despair.

Sophie, going between two rooms, cried over the bannister, so that the two women drinking tea in the kitchen could hear her, 'Don't worry, Miss Troll! The gate-house is yours – I'm giving it to you. You are to have fifty pounds a week pension from today on' . . .

The next room that Sophie went into was the music room . . . How beautiful it looked with the sun shining in and the rosewood piano uncovered for the first time. It was locked. Sophie found the key on the mantelpiece, under the portrait of a beautiful young woman who bore a striking resemblance to Mrs Maida as she might have looked sixty years before . . . Sophie's hand moved at random over the keyboard – ah, now she would be able to have lessons; she could well afford it! . . . The notes roused echoes all over the upper storey of the big house. There were music sheets in the piano stool, with the name 'Sunniva Maida' written in round immature script.

Sophie kissed the plaster cheek of Chopin.

Two hundred and fifty thousand, five hundred and twenty- one pounds and three pence . . . That's how much Sophie was worth, since an hour ago. 'Apart from the Hall and all the grounds and outhouses, and furnishings and objects of art and all appurtenances whatsoever belonging to the Hall, I leave and bequeath the residue of my estate to the girl Sophie Birsay: in the fair hope that, after such a long winter, she will bring April into a dead house and, after April, a long long summer filled with song, blossom, and the laughter of children, for many generations' . . .

The voice of the little lawyer, unused to such poetry in the documents he handled, paused to say, 'The late Mrs Maida's own words . . . The residue of the estate, after the deduction of all taxes, duties, fees, and expenses, amounts to £250,521:3. In due course, a cheque for that amount will be sent to the young lady I see sitting before me.'

He had given Sophie a thin conspiratorial smile . . .

Poor Miss Troll still sat, petrified by the thunderbolt. Her mother had managed to say, 'A cup of tea will do us all a world of good' . . .

A teapot and six cups and saucers! Sophie leaned over the bannister rail. 'Mother, I will get a golden teapot specially for you. I appoint you housekeeper here in the Hall. Your salary will be one hundred pounds a week . . .'

Whispers down below, in the kitchen, and the clink of cups. More tea had been brewed, obviously. There would be an ocean of tea in that kitchen before nightfall!

Sophie found herself in the room of death before she was aware of it. Here Mrs Maida had endured the last thirty years of her life. Here, three weeks ago, she had died.

Sophie threw open the window. The gardeners, Sam and Willie, were already beginning to clear the choked burn. She could actually hear the first singing of the waters. Soon there would be a little blue lake under the sycamore tree, reflecting the birds and leaves of summer.

Sophie opened a cupboard and found bundles of letters tied with red ribbons. Someone, far back in time, had loved Mrs Maida . . .

Ah, the excitement of the day had wrung Sophie dry! As she went down the wide stairway – *her* stairway, in *her* vast house – to get a cup of tea before the teapot was dry, she heard the music from the music room: wistful, delicate, heart-breaking, yet it trembled (lingering) on the verge of an all-but-impossible promise.

Pace Eggs

They woke, all three, and remembered, through the lingering shadows and images of sleep, that it was Saturday, and no school.

It was the day between Good Friday and Easter – the day for the gathering of eggs at all the island crofts.

They crammed their porridge and toast into their mouths. 'Have patience!' their mother chided them.

Their father had sailed his fishing boat *Hoy Lass* out west two hours ago, while Tom and Inga and Jamie still slept.

Their mother had laid out three small baskets for them, lined with straw and wool plucked from the fences.

Tom looked through the window and saw groups of children drifting across the hill a mile away, with baskets and pails.

'There'll be no eggs left,' he shouted, and fairly hurled himself into the coat his mother was holding out. 'Hurry! Come on!'

Scarfed and bonneted, Tom and Inga and Jamie passed into the cold morning, each carrying a basket.

The island had still a wintry look. There were scars of snow on the hill. In a field here and there it was difficult to tell whether a grey lump was a sheep or old lingering snow.

Tom knocked shyly at the open door of the first croft, Barnstead. 'Come in,' called a hearty voice. It did the children good to look into the ruddy face of Mrs Wilson.

The living-room was bright with four smiles. 'Eggs, is it?' cried Mrs Wilson. 'Pace eggs. The fisherman's bairns, are you? Let me see, Tom and Inga and Jamie. You've come at a good time. The hens have been laying like mad all week – they must have known you were coming.' Mrs Wilson went into a whitewashed room where she made butter and cheese, and came back and put an egg into each outstretched palm. And the eggs were warm. The children laid them carefully in their baskets. They heard the shouts of boys outside, on the wind. As they were leaving, Mrs Wilson said, 'It's always good for a croft, and the fields and animals too, when children come for the Pace eggs' . . .

Round the shoulder of the hill they came on a poor ruckle of stones that might have been a derelict shepherd's hut; but smoke was blowing from the chimney and a few hens strutted and dipped around the walls.

'Not here!' said Inga. 'We won't call here. Bill the old sailor lives here. He's crazy. He throws stones at the postman and the social security man. We'll go round it.'

But Tom went up to the old sailor's warped door, and knocked resolutely.

Jamie's heart fluttered inside him like a bird. The door slowly creaked open.

'Eggs, is it?' said the old sailor in the cosmopolitan accent that all deep-sea sailors have. 'Eggs and boys. And a girl. I've had a dozen greedy impudent boys and lasses at this door since daybreak. No peace, no peace. Look how you've frightened the hens. Are you Jock the fisherman's bairns? I thought so. Why can't you stay at home and eat fish, eh? I'm an old sailor. I'm cold. I'm hungry. Nobody in this island likes me. Why can't you leave me alone? Little beggars. I'm going to get a dog – a collie – with a loud sharp mouth. I was at school with your grandfather that died, old Andrew Garth. Wait, I'll give you something.'

Old Bill disappeared into the cobwebbed gloom of his house. Three cold blue hands, outside, hung in the wind. Old Bill reappeared, and with great care placed a round pebble in each palm: three sea washed stones.

Then the old sailor began to wheeze. He wheezed and hooted with such a gale of mirth that tears ran down his peatdark cheeks and he had to hold on to the door handle.

They heard his laughter from the far side of the burn. Tom and Inga had thrown their stones against his wall. Jamie looked long at his stone, as if it was a jewel from the ocean depths; then he put it in his pocket. The stone was more beautiful than any egg, in his opinion.

The next croft they came to was called Brandhurst, where a young couple lived who had just been married in January. The wonder of love was still in Gladys's eyes as she opened the door to them. 'Tom and Inga and Jamie,' she cried. 'Come for Pace eggs! Oh, shame on me. There isn't an egg in the whole house. Douglas and me, we've been so busy with the house and barn and byre, we've had no time to think about hens. Next year, when you come, there'll be a red and white flock round the door. There'll be two eggs for each of you, next Easter. Yes, there will. Come in, come in out of the cold. Your faces are grey. Come over beside the fire.'

They ate Gladys's gingerbread and drank ginger ale till warmth branched through their veins. They stood like young trees waiting to put out first leaves to the sun.

As they left Brandhurst they could hear Douglas chiding his second-hand tractor in the yard. 'Broke down again, have you, you slut! You wait, the horses are biding their time. Old Peg the mare never let my father down . . .' And Gladys stood on the doorstep, waving blessings after them, and promising six big brown eggs next March, for sure.

There, near the crossroads, they met four frowning boys from the other end of the island, all older than them, and enemies too, for children from the sea village rarely mix with children from the hill. (But, after a few years, they get on tolerably well with each other.)

Now Raymond the son of Ned the shepherd blocked their path. The baskets of the hill boys were half full of white and brown eggs, and a few larger pale green duck eggs.

'Let's see what you've got,' said Raymond.

They held out their baskets. Raymond whispered, as if in awe. 'One egg each! The little fish-folk have got one egg apiece' . . . He turned to his three companions, and suddenly they were all shaken with contemptuous laughter. 'One egg each!' they cried. 'A solitary egg for the little fish-folk.'

Tom and Inga and Jamie scuttled like rabbits down a side road, while the hill boys were still helpless and falling against each other with scorn. 'One egg!' . . . 'The little fish-folk'. They bent double at the crossroads, useless with mirth.

Tom and Inga and Jamie, very grave, crossed the bridge over the burn, and saw below them the wide fertile wedge of land where the big farms were.

There they took a good harvest of eggs. At one or two farms they got a curt reception, or a silent reception, but most of the farm-wives threw their doors wide at sight of the little fish-folk (children are loved by the farmers and their wives; they are a greater joy to them even than a golden field of barley in August. One here and there has had a spirit eaten and eroded by the other gold: money.) At all the farms they were given eggs, large or small, and here and there they got a bannock and cheese to eat, or a slice of cherry cake, or a cup of milk.

Soon their baskets were so full of Pace eggs that they had to be careful where they set new offerings. They had to structure the fragile things with utmost care. Gently they bore their cargoes from the last door.

It was time to be getting home. Their baskets would hold not a single egg more. Jamie was very tired – he dragged his feet; they had traversed the island from end to end. Never had their baskets been so brimming. 'If only that Raymond Gloup could meet us now!' said Tom.

At that moment disaster struck. Jamie, trailing along behind Tom and Inga, and very weary, stuck his foot against a stone on the road. He measured his length in the dust – his basket flew out of his hand – eighteen eggs fell and smashed; if some band of tramps had been there, a pan and a driftwood fire, they'd have had the most wonderful omelette.

After a first gape of wonderment, Jamie struggled to his feet. His whole body grew rigid with misery and chagrin. He covered his face with his hands, but the water-drops glittered between his fingers.

Raymond and the three hill-boys had seen the accident from the high farm of Linklater nearby. They began to laugh again; and their black mockery, worse than before, pierced the fisherman's children. 'No eggs for the small fish-folk! Nothing but seaweed, limpets, salt for the small fish-folk!'

That salt in his wounds, Jamie wept even more bitterly.

Tom and Inga tried to comfort him. They had plenty of eggs in their two baskets – Jamie would get a third share.

'No,' said Jamie, who could be quite stubborn. 'It was my fault. Just leave me alone.'

Inga gave a cry – she pointed. There, into the bay and the harbour, came their father's fishing boat, *Hoy Lass*; they looked, and saw the three fish baskets alive with silver, and a long loud waver of gulls following the boat.

'That's the biggest catch of the year so far!' said Tom. And he and Inga ran helter-skelter down the brae to meet their father when he tied up his boat at the pier. The two were careful, all the same, to put their hands over their delicate country cargoes, the Pace eggs.

Jamie was left behind with his bruised knees and palms. He sat in the ditch in utter abject misery. The world was a dead wintry place; all the lingering cruelty of winter pierced him through and through. His sister and brother had deserted him. The world was as dead as the stone in his pocket.

How long Jamie sat in the ditch beside his ruined egg-hoard, I don't know. His face was as tight as a fist with misery. He was ashamed to go through the village with an empty basket, and bruises, and tear-stains. The old women in the doors would be sure to ask what ailed him – had a farm dog bitten him? Had the coarse hill boys beaten him up and robbed him? Jamie could not endure those old wintry mouths.

Once Jamie opened his eyes, and he saw an amazing thing in the ditch an arm's-stretch away. It was a daisy, the first daisy he had seen that year. The daisy held its modest torch just above the dead grass, and shed a small brightness on the cold grey afternoon.

'A daisy,' said Jamie. 'What's a daisy? They'll soon be as common as stones and seagulls. Daisy – "day's eye", that's what it means, the teacher told us.'

And still he sat, his fists in his eyes, while the first daisy of the year held up into the wind the little pink-and-white flame it had been guarding in the underworld all winter.

It was beginning to be cold on the hillside. Jamie shivered. When the sun was down and the lamps were lit in the village windows, then it would be a good time for him to go home, safe from the mockery of the village children and the old wintry mouths.

Jamie opened his eyes again. One planet – the evening star – glittered coldly above the hill. Now there were two brightnesses in the world, of the earth and of the air. But no, when Jamie looked again the daisy was still there in the ditch beside him; but now it had closed its eye, having a dewy heaviness on it. It would open its eye again to the greater eye of day, the sun, on Easter morning.

The first daisy – the first star. With a sudden lightening of the heart Jamie was up and out of the ditch and he was running as hard as he could towards the cluster of lamps that was the village.

Everybody was indoors beside the fires. He was free on the island road, running, beyond reach of inquisition or mockery.

He ran, and ran, and his face glowed, but his cold hands and torn knees yearned for the leaping flames of the hearth-fire.

When finally he flung open the door, there the family was at the table, having their supper of fried haddocks and barley bread: his mother, and Tom and Inga . . . But where was the good fisherman? Where was his father?

'Your father saw you running', said his mother. 'He has something for you. Jamie, you're blue with cold! – Come and stand beside the fire.'

The bright peat flames laved him, with yellow dapplings, a shifting net.

Then the door opened and the fisherman came in. From his forefinger depended another brightness, a small Atlantic haddock. 'For you, Jamie,' said the fisherman gravely. 'Something out of the sea for your supper.'

And so, with that last sea brightness, the winter was over and done for Jamie and for the whole island. He was caught up in a green gathering wave of grass and daffodils, larks and herring-shoals, that would presently break over the bewintered world.

And the hearth-flames were the sun, a small sun-gift that the sun bestowed on the children of men, to be a comfort and a delight to them.

Anna's Boy

There was a child, a boy, up at the croft of Auding; everybody knew that, but nobody in the island had seen him. Not once.

Nell the howdie wife had seen him, the day he was born four years ago, but Nell was in the kirkyard two winters now.

Anna the mother was strange. Nobody crossed her threshold, neither neighbour nor the cousin from the far end of the island, he that had the big farm and might have been glad to help her and the child: if not with money, then with eggs, butter, tatties and smoked bacon. She wanted nothing to do with him and his charity.

Sometimes an inquisitive soul would make an attempt to see the child. Anna couldn't stay indoors always. She had to go sometimes to see to her two sheep, and to the grocery van that stopped at the end of the road every Friday morning.

Three times Bella Scad tried to get into the house to see the child, when Anna was at field or well or van. And three times the door was locked! A door locked! – such a thing had never been known in the island before. The queer lass had turned the key in the lock and put it in her apron pocket before leaving the house.

Bella Scad pressed her face against the pane. There was no sign of the bairn inside: her eyes saw nothing but the interior of a very poor house, without a single ornament on the mantelpiece or a picture on the wall. All the needful things were there, girnal and lamp and spinning-wheel and kettle and pot and a little fire of peats blinking on the hearth. But no child – there was no boy to be seen or heard. As Bella Scad squashed her face still harder against the pane, a cold voice behind her said, 'Are you wanting something?'

It was Anna, come back from the grocery van too soon with her few messages.

For once in her life the gossip and tale-bearer was lost for words. 'I was just wondering . . . if thu were all right . . . for I havena seen thee for a day or two . . .'

'When I need you,' said Anna, 'I'll send for you.'

And with that Bella Scad slunk off like a chidden dog, and Anna turned the key in her door and went inside.

Of course, there were all sorts of rumours about the boy. He was misshapen, he was an idiot, he was blind, he was a deaf-mute. For one or other of those reasons Anna didn't let the boy over the door. There was one very wicked old man who lived on the far side of the hill. 'He's maybe dead,' said this cruel old creature one winter night in the smithy, 'and buried in the peatmoss.'

The men who gathered for news and discussion in the smithy every evening were so shocked that there was silence for a while. Then Thomasina Brett the blacksmith's wife cried from the door between smithy and house, 'I heard a bairn's voice from Anna's place no later than yesterday, when I was going down to the shore. Shame on you!'

The smithy debaters turned black looks on the wicked old man. And he slunk away into the night, and never came back for a month.

Bridie the tinker lass said she had seen the boy, one day when Anna was at the well with her bucket. The door stood open – Bridie had gone in. 'He was more like an angel than a bairn,' said Bridie. (But Bridie was forever seeing ghosts, trows, mermaids.)

Still there was much talk in the village and in the farms about Anna and her child that no one had ever clapped eyes on.

'I tell you what,' said Roberta Manson at the WRI meeting, when the ladies were nibbling their dainties and sipping their tea, 'once Anna's boy turns five, he'll have to come out and be seen. The law of the land says every child must go to school at the age of five' . . . The island ladies nodded sagely over the tea-cups. Anna wouldn't be able to hide her bairn away for ever. One day next August the boy would have to go to the village school with his satchel under his arm.

But Anna's boy did not go to school next August, among the little flock of new 'scholars', boys and girls, all mute with the wonderment of blackboard, slate pencils, coloured chalks, wall-charts, map of the whole world, and Miss Carmichael who was both kind and severe.

Anna's boy was where he had always been, at home.

Of course enquiries were made. The school attendance officer knocked at Anna's door, and got no reply. He pressed the sneck – the door was locked. Mr Smith the general merchant who was the island representative on the education committee called. The door opened. Anna's cold face looked into his. No, said she, the bairn wouldn't be going to the school. If Mr Smith wanted more information, let him ask Dr Fergusson. Smith the grocer tried to look over Anna's shoulder. There was no boy to be seen. But over the mantelpiece a picture was pinned – a crude child's picture, in coloured crayons, of a flower, but such a flower as Mr Smith had never seen in Orkney or in any place he had visited, ever. The flower enriched the poor room.

Then Mr Smith found himself standing outside in the cold. For Anna had shut the door against him.

*   *   *

'Oh yes,' said Dr Fergusson to Smith the merchant, 'I've seen the boy – of course I've seen him. He's a delicate child. No point in him going to school now that winter's setting in. Never be able to trudge through snow, in the teeth of gales. Impossible. Maybe in spring, at daffodil time, he could give the school a try, to see how things go then.' Yes, by all means Dr Fergusson would write out a certificate . . .

So, it seemed the appearance of Anna's boy would be postponed for a while yet.

Two days before Christmas there was a school party. What excitement! The severe schoolroom was suddenly an enchanted cavern, hung with decorations and murals the children had made themselves. The desks had been pushed into a corner to make way for a long trestle, and it was loaded with sandwiches, cakes with icing and marzipan and spice and sultanas, and with pyramids of oranges and apples, and ranked bottles of lemonade. And there was a Christmas tree that glittered with coloured lights: the first illuminated Christmas tree ever seen in the island (for electric power had only come the previous autumn.)

And the twenty school-children were there in their best suits and dresses, and they made as much noise as any crowd at the Lammas Fair; except that their cries were purer and sweeter. And, on this evening, Miss Carmichael made no attempt to restrain them.

Outside, a wind from the Atlantic howled about the school, and from time to time showers of hail crashed against the tall school windows.

But the storm served only to increase the merriment inside.

Until, suddenly, the whole school went dark! The babble ceased abruptly. A small girl began to cry. There were other whimpers here and there.

'It's all right,' said the voice of Miss Carmichael out of the darkness. 'It's just a power cut. The lights will come on again. Find your desks and sit down. It looks as if I'll have to go into the school-house and look for our old paraffin lamps. I hope I can find them. I hope there's some paraffin in the cupboard' . . .

But Miss Carmichael didn't sound too sure; and there was a fresh outburst of sobs and wails from some of the shadowy pupils groping among the hard shadows of desks.

The outer door opened. A butterfly of light entered, and went wavering down the corridor between the rows of desks. Then it was petals, a folded flower of light. It lingered beside the Christmas tree, and hung over it at last, steadfast and tranquil, a star.

Miss Carmichael and the twenty glimmering pupils were silent.

'I'm Anna's boy,' said the stranger who had carried the lighted candle through the storm.

The Twentieth of August

Feast of St Bernard,
Anno Domini 1183.

There they stood, six or seven men, under the red shadow.
They had set down burdens at their feet.

The man beside the candle said, 'Let the first offering be brought.'

How he shuffled and hirpled through that big cave, more awesome than any sea cave, old Thorf, out of the web of red shadows into the candle-glim, with a straw basket on his shoulder that he clasped with both bone-bright hands. There hung about him the fish smell, that was stronger than the lingering sweet-smelling cloud (now dispersed). The cod glimmered in the candle light. The old man laid his basket of cod on the stone.

He went down, a painful kneeling. He turned him about. And the net of shadows took him. Thorf stood in peace under the thick pillar.

'Let the next offering be brought.'

A small thick man – his basket too he carried on his shoulder. (Ah, the loneliness of the hill, it was different from the loneliness of this place. And the midsummer peat-cutting sun, it was different from the one candle that struggled in a small draught. The laird's man was not so awesome as this priest.) He thumped the basket of black peat on the stone.

The priest bowed.

The peat-man could not get to his place fast enough. Half way back to his folk, he remembered where he was. Slowly he drifted out of the moth-light.

'The next offering.'

A young man, dark as a Pict, blue-black curls all round his face. And he carried in his arms a small clay jar. He stumbled into the light, then stopped, then half-turned back. Whispers behind him, 'Go on, Magnus' . . . 'Go under the bones of Magnus the saint' . . . 'Take strength from the martyr' . . . And after, the young man Magnus went forward bravely. He set the jar of ground oats beside the gifts of cod and peat. But he would not look at the priest. But bent his knee and turned away fast. Returning, he touched with a finger the pier where the bones were.

Now their eyes, that had had sea-dazzle in them all morning since they had pushed out the boat *Tern* from the beach at Rackwick, were growing accustomed to the glooms and gleams of this immense cave.

The solemness of the priest did not frighten them so much. They could see that he was an old man. He murmured like the grandfathers in the valley, yet not familiarly; he seemed to use tongue and lips and teeth and throat and 'the roof of the mouth' as if he were performing ancient solemn music upon an ancient instrument.

'The next offerer, will he now come forward?'

The next offerer was hardly more than a boy. (Or was it a girl? The offerer could have been a girl, there was so much blown blond hair athwart the eyes and down about the shoulders, there was so much trout-pink and seapink on the cheeks.) It was a boy – and now that the candle light was on him the few blond hairs on the upper lip could be seen. (The woman and the girls were all safe in the valley that day.) Yet the offerer should have been a woman, perhaps, for didn't the young women see to the bees, the hives, the combs? The boy set a small pot of honey beside the stone. And he looked up from his knees at the priest, a smile kindling in the candle flame. And the old priest gave him a withered puckering of the lips, and raised his hand, dismissing the boy in peace.

A harsh whisper when the boy got back among the valley men. 'You were too brazen! There should have been more reverence. What am I to say to your mother?' . . . The boy's flurry of whispers was drowned in the half-sung summons, 'The next gift now' . . .

Thomas of Quernstones was either so frightened or so burdened that they had to push him out from the pillar. And once out in the side-aisle, so much hay hung over his face that he blundered like a blind man, here and there. He dripped dry grass. With every step he took, wisps and dry flowers fell on to the floor. Even a bee broke out of the blond fog, the shagginess, and went buzzing among shadows and statues, and Thomas stood there, lost. At last he dragged some straw from the straw cowl over his eyes. Then he could see the priest and the candle. He staggered forward quickly and set the bale down, with its hundred whisperings, among the other gifts. 'A mouthful or two for the bishop's horse,' he said to the priest.

The priest bowed.

Thomas, stuck here and there, head to foot, with pieces of hay, went back smiling among the pillars.

(And who would clean all that Rackwick grass from the floor? There were men who did that job. They had heard that.)

'I will accept another offering.'

Another jar went forward, borne on the shoulder of a

creature that looked more like a scarecrow than a man, he was so crooked and ragged. This jar contained a liquid, some thick sluggish fluid. Moreover it had an ugly smell among the smells of beeswax and incense. It was oil from the livers of fish: it might do for the students of the cathedral song-school on a winter night, or for some deacon or other as he turned a lonely midnight page. The oil slurped in the jar and made a surly glug-glug as the offerer set it down.

It was approved. It was accepted. The priest raised his hand.

A boy appeared silent and vested from somewhere at the back of the church. He lit a new candle from the guttering stump in the candle-stick, and replaced the one with the other. And went off another way, in white whispers of linen.

'There is yet one more gift.'

What an agitated whispering then among the great red pillars! – shufflings, whisperings, urgings, denials. Something was amiss with the seventh offerer and the seventh offering.

The priest lingered at the altar's edge, peered out, hesitated, then descended and came slowly up the side aisle towards the men from the sea valley. Old Thorf of Moorfea went half way to meet the priest, hobbling and grunting on his one good leg.

The two old men met mid-way. The priest bowed. Thorf's words drowned the whispered query of the priest. 'It's Ronald the shepherd,' he said. 'He should have been here, with his fleece. He should have come with the rest of us. Oh no, he had never been to Kirkvoe before – he must see the sights – he must go here, there, and everywhere. Last I saw him, Father, he was going down to look at the boats on the beach, with his rolled-up sheepskin on his shoulder. *What kind of fishing boats do the men hereabouts have?* he wondered . . . And that's the last we've seen of Ronald the shepherd' . . .

'He will come in his own good time,' said the priest.

'I only hope, Father,' said old Thorf, 'he hasn't gone into an ale-house and sold the fleece for a drink. It's a good fleece. We should have taken it from him.'

At that moment there was a disturbance at the door of St Magnus, and a man came in, panting as if he had run all the way from Birsay or Hamnavoe. 'I'm here!' he cried between gasps. 'Kirkvoe's a big place, I know that now. I lost my way. Don't tell me I'm late!'

They gave him angry looks.

Thorf shook his fist at Ronald.

The priest smiled. He returned to the altar. The new candle-flame laved the puckerings and wrinkles of his face, and his silver hair.

Ronald went forward reverently and knelt and laid the sheepskin beside the other offerings.

Later the Rackwick men brought in oars and a sail and three creels, a plough and twelve sickles and quernstones, and a peat-spade.

The priest blessed them.

Later the priest said Mass, and people from the farms and ships came in and stood among the Rackwick men. They knelt. They rose again. The altar-boy made answer for them. *In principio erat verbum.* The Mass was over.

The Rackwick men got home under the first star.

2

The 20th day of the 8th month, 1283 AD.

There appeared horsemen riding from Hamnavoe upon the roads north and east: Scotsmen.

A Scottish horseman came betwixt the 2 hills called The Wart and Coolag, into that tunship callit Rackwick. And cries this Scotsman, making a trumpet of his hands, 'Whom wad ye hae for King, England or Norway? The English should they come would make a ravelment of the fair-set loom of liberties, but the little white rose that it is to be Scotland's queen grows even now in the fair garden of Norway.'

The folk of Rackwick looked at the herald as they would upon a loud simpleton, and put once more twenty sickles into the rigs.

3

1383 – the XX day in August.

To his grace the Earl of Kirkwall, in the Castell there. May it please your grace.

In the darkness of last night came sudden and secret upon that shore of Hoy called Rackwick, sundry sheep thieves from Caithness in the country of Scotland, who bore away sheep to the number of twenty, all the people in the valley being asleep but Simon Sigurdson. Simon Sigurdson being estranged from his good wife sleeps but ill of late, and he heard after midnight what he deemed well to be the cry of Bella his old ewe down by the shore, as it were in distress. Taking his staff in his hand he heard what seemed to be a fold of unquiet sheep out in the bay: a delusion that one might suppose in a drunken dream. Simon laid hold on the shadowy arm of a man at the shore and asked what the outcry of sheep might mean on the ocean, and got for reply a mighty stroke upon his head that enveloped him in multitudinous stars and a deeper darkness. He woke up with a bruise upon his temple and his legs awash in the rising flood-tide. Five crofters have lost sheep, including (alas) Simon Sigurdson's Bella, that trotted so well at his heels.

4

Haven fallen through the
time glass of anno domini
1483, of the grains of sand
we call days, two hundred
and thirty three.

Time hasteth on.

A small handful under a red rock: it sifts through the fingers. This we call the life of a man.

In this place, look how their lives are circumscribed by immensities of red cliff, and the infinite sea.

Thankful am I to be come among you at last, a wandering one with cowl and cord about my middle. A poor man among poor men.

Of your charity, give me a crust and a small fish.

I have made a cup of my hands, for to take water up out of the stream that you have here. Ah, how the sweet cold drops spill between my fingers, like blessed souls in the blue air.

Know: I have passed through this town and that in the kingdom of Scotland. I lingered at the door of the king's castle, there the king sat, with silks about his withering flesh, and gold upon that head that is soon to be a skull. And I saw how there flowed past the king's throne a sweet-smelling river of men, merchants and captains and lairds and knights, and one and all they had stitched smiling masks upon their faces, and one after other they went down upon their knees, and they gave into the hand of the golden one scrolls of parchment with seals upon them.

And the king gave those rolled-up pleadings and flatterings into the keeping of an old courtier who piled them upon a silver platter that stood upon an oak table.

Each sought advancement. Each knight and laird and merchant, each smirked for place and preferment: before they have their corruption closed up forever in a carved stone.

And I saw in other streets and wynds of the city folk with blue thin faces and bare stitches [rags] about them.

And women stood in the vennels, speaking bitter words.

And children went, making bird-prints in the snow.

Yea, and my lord the abbot went into a locked chamber of purer gold and jewels of emerald and lapis lazuli beyond any royal treasure: many a day before those stones are dust! I had cold looks in that abbey, as I sat at their table with my wooden bowl and spoon.

I fared north. A shepherd would put a handful of oats into his pot.

To you also – before I break this piece of fish and this round of bread – I will recite one of the songs of Francis, who taught us to imitate the poverty of Christ: He, being most poor, yet had in His keeping the infinite treasures of earth and heaven.

The sun shines on your patches of corn today. (Your fare is simple and good in the mouth.) Listen: I will sing the hymn of our brother Francis to the sun.

Yea, and the sun is but golden dust too. It sufficeth for our brief dances.

I have dipped fingers in the water. Listen. I will make of my mouth a trembling harp.

5

20th day of August, 1583, AD.

As our ship *Hermione* drew to shore, but still well out in the bay, I saw through my glass how the people of this part of

Hoy drove their cattle, sheep, and pigs before them to the gorge of a dark valley, in utmost flurry and haste, doubtless fearing us to be a pirate vessel. We went ashore in the longboat, Sven and Swartz and Neilsen and some others, who drew seven firkins of water from two wells that were there. The huts of the inhabitants were most miserably appointed. The floors were of mud and the interior of the one hut our men visited full of blue choking fumes of turf. One very old woman sat in a chair among this reek, who rose and seemed to greet us courteously enough, tho' we could understand no word of her speech. Swartz laid a crown piece upon her table. It seemed to our crew-men that the hills were full of eyes, as we rowlocked and plied the oars.

6

20th day of August, 1683.

This day my wife interviewed four island women for the task of housekeeper at the Manse of Hoy. Three answered sensibly and demurely, and left. Last came this comely lass from Rackwick in the west, who spoke no word to Mistress McVey at all but addressed all her remarks to me, such as: 'I will make you very sweet butter,' and 'The washings I wash are whiter than snow, after the sun and wind have had their way,' and 'I will shave your face in the morning after breakfast, and you are to take a penny from my wages for every scratch I scratch with the razor on your bonny face,' and 'The fires I light for you in your library! – you will like winter better than summer.' I do not know how long the innocent lovely creature would have prattled on, but in the midst of her torrent of promisings my wife gave her a curt dismissal. She hissed like a snake and spat on the doorstep and was gone. I see this Eve in the kirk on a Sabbath now and again.

7

August – twentieth day – 1783.

The brig wrecked in thick fog under Rora Head. There were such surges of sea that day, that the vessel quickly broke up, and but two sailors scaled the crag, one of whom expired from cold and exhaustion soon after. A lad of twelve years or thereby we resuscitated with kneadings, pulsings at his ribs, breath-minglings, and the fire at Bunnertoon. He had no English, he gave us to understand his name was Anton Zervoovich (or something like) and that the name of the ship was *Dansick*, America bound with furs and Russian spirits, also that his father was master of the vessel. After that, he wept a little, but composed himself soon, and (kneeling) murmured and made crosses before his face and breast and Jane wrapt him in a blanket in the box-bed where he slept beyond a round of the clock. This boy Anton was sent on to Leith on the *Thomasina*, out of Hamnavoe, to the Baltic consul there. I much regret to say: two hogsheads of that spirit called Vodka were saved out of a hundred or so, since when no work has been done in the harvest field except by the raging women of this valley. There have been two fights in Moorfea and at the shore on account of this vodka. Willie of Ruemin fell crossing the burn, very intoxicated, and broke an arm. I fear there may be other barrels of that same eau-de-vie of the Steppes concealed in some cave or fissure of the rocks. If so, it will be a lurid and fishless winter here in Hoy. Seven bodies have been found and given Christian interment. There needs a lighthouse upon some part of the shore of this island. (Even as I write, word has been brought me that some Rackwick women have smelt out a spirit barrel from the wreck, in a bay called Little Rackwick, that is set between crags on the way to Melsetter and Long Hope, and with great stones they broke open the barrel and let the contents gush out in a grey flood: which, being reported in the valley, Willie of the broken arm cursed and wept beside his fire.)

8

20th day of August, 1883.

Sara has gone to the Lammas Fair in Kirkwall on the fishing boat *Raven*, with fifty-one grey knitted jumpers and twenty pair of socks and mittens, and six blue bonnets with ear warmers, and 6 gravats from the moorit sheep. Oh, but my fingers and the fingers of Liza and Ellen were furrowed and bone-bright and in spasms with a summer of knitting! And Sara came back yesterday with 2 sovrans in her purse, two crowns, 7 half crowns, 3 florins, 12 shillings, and copper like a fist-ful of mud. Sam and Tom our men are looking ashamed of themselves, shaking their heads and spitting. Their fish fetch a penny here and there, nothing more. Sara whispered to old Liza that a nice farm boy from Abune-the-Hill in Birsay had kissed her outside a stall selling apples and toffee. This seemed to please the creature more than the treasures she had brought home. Well content, we set out in the evening to bring home baskets of peat from the cuttings beyond Ruemin but were sore tormented by midgies near sunset till a sea breeze got up.

9

20/8/83.

Stromness suddenly buttoned itself into a coat of mist. Passing the west lighthouse of Graemsay, the sun glimmed out like a tarnished sixpence. Beyond, the Hoy hills with

muted sun on them. Seven or eight tourists climbed on to
the pier of Moness. The car went on in increasing light. If
Orkney (I thought) was a collection of books: Birsay and
Orphir the sagas, Egilsay the saint's book, Kirkwall the
ledger of accounts and records, Stromness an anthology of
shanties and whaling stories, this part of Hoy is the book of
lyrics. We climbed the sheep path to Bunnertoon, the
highest house, which of late years has been a workshop
of music. We sat on a stone block outside the door and
drank coffee. A warm wind blew off the sea. The minuscule
iridescent dense droplets of haar hid the Pentland Firth and
the Atlantic to the west, and lay in the folds of the hills and
crag fissures, and put a grey gate across the mouth of the
valley. To forget the hardness of the stone seat, I took pen
to the reporter's notebook I sometimes carry, and in the
blank dwam or seance out of which some writers summon
images and rhythms, I imagined nine centuries of this day
(August the 20th), in the 83rd year of the nine centuries;
and the little episodes tumbled over themselves to get
written, to be shuttled on to the loom of the imagination.
(I leave history to the hard stone-breakers and stone
dressers and stone-setters who know how to build solid
houses.) Those 'prose poems' are but blown scents and
gossamer strands; they may give a passing pleasure. What
shall Rackwick, or Orkney, or the world be in August 2083?
. . . Friends climbed up from Mucklehoose and Noust in
the late afternoon with plastic containers of dark home-
brewed ale. We sat and reclined on blankets on the grass,
and laughed and told stories and swilled the dark enchantment till the sun went down behind Moorfea: yet the great
cliffs that enclose the valley on the south – the Kist, Craig-
Gate, The Sneuk – were pillars of fire for a while yet. Sheep
nudged the fence, and drifted by. Our friends went away.

Presently the cottage brimmed with stereo music and smells of steak and sausages frying. This Rackwick puts a great hunger on its thralls.

During the night rain beat on the roof. There were five or six stabs of lighting that (half drowsed) I took to be flashes of a lighter-buoy out in the Pentland.

10

Dies 232 an. 2083 2105 hrs.

52843 X

712

mackerel, 5 boats out, wind ENE force 2/3

W53YA0620173A

sea samples d.230, nucl nil

d.238, sheep fleecing. Five sheep have not been seen since d.194. Reft, cliff-fallen? Moorfea, beyond the ridge, skull bones a ravel of wool, skua-prey.

T83535

The under-horizon Greenland ship sighted d.222 has seen well to the shoals. We have 32 mackerel out of 5 boats.

WCX

The official fr. Kirkuvagr d.231. *It may be, we shall be able to put the sickles among the oats about that season day hangs with night in perfect equipoise, when in the loom light-grey thread meshes exactly with dark-grey thread, when so to speak bucket comes from burn half full of the blue-and-silver tremors of time: then it may be we shall go among such ears as are with sickle and with scythe, and gleaners following.*

The young man spoke words and numbers into the machine he keeps in his pocket and made haste to go from this valley of madness.

WT046Z

Thurso a glow-worm cluster. Empty orb of Dounreay maketh answer to the fulling orb of Luna.

Burdened sheep moon-silvered dew-drenched, the children will make circles (wild shouting flings) about your mild errancies in five days or in six days, for to make a fluttering frightened congress of you, for the men of this valley S352/H to shear burdensome grey fleece-fogs from you. Ho, Mister Blackface, woo't please you, the fire o' the sun burning hot in the House of Harvest, yield your coat to this boy?

(I sit in a wooden hut near Bunnertoon, set high, making computer calculations that are required daily for Min. Ag/ Fisc files in office MQ3 at Kirkuvagr – loc 0358/K. I am forbid to touch oar or plough or peat or fleece, so elevated my calling above the swarm of toilers below. There remain 133 sheets of ancient greenish paper, saved (who knows how?) from a school that was anciently here. On a sheet, now and again, parsimonious as mouse or miser, I put down a few flourishes and quaint phrases out of a lost language, for to keep in some sense my wits whole and kempt and clean. At the end of ream and writing, a cleaner fire shall go through all.

I have set myself a sacred task for next winter, the naming of the five fishing boats.

Midnight. The isle is full of noises: as (now)

    W83LVBTR

    00015 8

    ZZ 8D/L 1983

The Corn and the Tares

1

A small island in Orkney produced two of the most famous poets in the north, though seven and a half centuries separate them. That Wyre island should produce two poets would be sufficiently remarkable, but it is likely that Bjarni Kolbeinson and Edwin Muir lived under the same roof – not literally, for many thatches must have been set and removed in the meantime, and new beams laid, and withered stones replaced by fresh-quarried stones. Bjarni Kolbeinson's father was the Norse chief of Wyre – Kolbein Hruga, a man of such heroic rages that they entered into legend. For centuries after Kolbein, mothers would threaten their unruly children, 'Cubbie Roo'll get thee'. Kolbein's son, Bjarni, became a priest, and was made bishop of Orkney in 1188. All we know of Bishop Bjarni is that during his episcopate he did good work on the still uncompleted Cathedral of Saint Magnus the Martyr in Kirkwall. In his time, too, St Magnus's newphew, Earl Rognvald Kolson, was canonized. Like St Rognvald, the bishop was a famous poet. Seemingly all that remains of his verse is the fragmentary *Lay of the Jomsvikings*. Into this narrative poem in the heroic style is woven a love-refrain: 'The göding's daughter has deadened my joy./ Of a mighty house is this worker of grief' . . . The story went that in his youth Bjarni had fallen in love with the daughter of an Orkney chieftain, but nothing came of it: 'That girl has taken all my laughter away' . . . 'She of the lovely hands has stunned me with grief' . . . 'On this poem for her I lavish my skill' . . . *The Lay of the Jomsvikings*, all about those lyrical outcries, is loud with battle-cry and sea-surge and the cleaving of skulls.

In the story, I imagine an earlier – a first – sweet-hearting for Bjarni.

A two-year-old child, Edwin Muir was brought to the farm of The Bu in Wyre in 1889, when his father became the tenant farmer there. That farm name, The Bu, goes right back to the early Norse settlement of Orkney: the chief man of every island and parish farmed The Bu.

The mind delights to dwell on those two poets, so far apart in time, breathing the same salt air and sitting perhaps at the same hearth-stone, and passing their 'angel-infancy' under that huge overarching sky. Certainly, in their childhood, they would have watched the sowing and the reaping of the same fields. It is in childhood, and among such scenes, that a poet is summoned.

> Call not thy wanderer home as yet
> > Though it be late.
> Now is his first assailing of
> > The invisible gate.
> Be still through that light knocking. The hour
> > Is thronged with fate.
>
> To that first tapping at the invisible door
> > Fate answereth.
> What shining image or voice, what sigh
> > Or honied breath
> Comes forth, shall be the master of life
> Even to death . . .

2

He knew that a poem was stirring inside him, feeling –
though blind and inarticulate still – its dazzling way through
the darkness: a rhythm, an uncertain pulsing, like a late
migrant bird lost now and bewildered for a moment, yet on
the true course, unerring. It would find its way. The light
grew a little, there was an image: the farm, horses, a
harvestfield . . .

Disappointing. Must he always return to the same few
images, again and again, the farm in Wyre, his father and his
cousin in Sutherland coming out of the barn with new-
sharpened scythes – the great plough-horse grazing in the
meadow – the sea glitter – himself a child – then evening in
the lamplight, his father solemnly turning the pages of the
bible to find a good text.

> The kingdom of heaven is likened unto a man which
> sowed good seed in his field. But while men slept, his
> enemy came and sowed tares among the wheat . . . 'Let
> both grow together until the harvest: and in the time of
> harvest I will say to the reapers 'Gather ye together first
> the tares, and bind them in bundles to burn them: but
> gather the wheat into my barn" . . .'

It was disconcerting, a little – he seemed in a way to be
writing the same poem over and over – he hadn't moved on
very far since he had written 'Horses', long long ago, in mid-
Europe in the nineteen-twenties.

It was, all the same, a constant delight, this turning back to
childhood and the island farm. From that source he drew his
strength: with that strength his imagination could voyage to
the world's edges.

It couldn't be helped. This new poem – if it comes at all (many a poem fluttered and fell, hollow-hearted, on the long journey) – would once more be about The Bu farm and the cornfields and the ripe winds of late summer . . . About, also, his own first sense of guilt and shame and pollution – Yes, for even as a child those dark shapes had moved through his mind, flawing the pure crystal. A mystery and a terror to a small boy. There was no one he could tell those things to. Who would understand? Perhaps he was the only flawed creature in the island, in Orkney, in all the world! He had only one foot in Eden. The other foot lingered, in terror, over an abyss of fear and guilt.

He took out his biro and wrote on the first piece of paper he could find on his desk – the back of a letter: 'One foot in Eden still I stand . . .' How did that sound? The image was good, the more his mind lingered on it. A gift, again; he couldn't have thought of it himself. The music of the line passable – oh, more than that, surely! . . . A rhyme for 'stand'. A score of rhymes fluttered faintly at the edge of his mind. 'Land'. A lot could be done with a basic word like that. It could be a field, a country, one of the four elements . . . 'And look across the other land'.

His biro made smudges on the paper as he wrote . . . 'My writing is more a spider-track than a stone heraldic motto,' he thought . . .

'The other land'? – What other land? The vast tract of time and history, man's sojourn on earth, exiled from Eden.

Would he be able to go on from there? Yes, he would. The poem was set, it was beginning to push up like a green cornshoot. He might finish it before the sun went down. It might, on the other hand, be a while in coming; all summer, maybe.

He was often tired nowadays, often unwell.

'The world's great day is wearing late . . .'

Another line! He wrote. The nearer he drew to death, the starker seemed those great mysterious absolutes and opposites of good and evil. Had he not lived through the most evil time in all the world's history – Hitler and the war and the holocaust – the very time that, his young generation had been assured, mankind, devoted to material achievement and enlightenment and progress, was about to cast off its chains for good?

He wrote, his biro scurrying over the page,

> 'Yet strange these fields that we have planted
> So long with crops of love and hate' . . .

A kind of ballad-beat. But – though he had tried to write that way once, long ago – he wasn't good at those stark dramatic image-sequences for which the old ballads were unsurpassed. He was a lyricist of flowing lines, not a story-teller.

Now the poetry was all about him, he couldn't stop it, it was like the flood-tide lapping the shores of Wyre island, rising higher and higher over stone and reef and rockpool. The regular urgent beat of incoming waves. The poet yielded himself to the poem with delight.

Rhyming was no difficulty. The rhymes came at him, inerrably. The poetical argument didn't falter for a moment. There was only, occasionally, the testing of this word and that in his mind, to discover which rang truer – no, more, the one only inevitable word.

> 'Nothing now can separate
> The corn and tares compactly grown,
> The armorial weed in stillness bound

> About the stalk; these are our own.
> Evil and good stand thick around
> In the fields of charity and sin
> Where we shall lead our harvest in . . .'

The rhymes chimed softly throughout the script, like muted bells. This was the way it ought to be: not like all the 'free verse' so common nowadays, that was held together by no such sweet constraints.

The poet lit another cigarette; another thread of smoke climbed up the the grey-blue hank of smoke over the desk.

The little island of his childhood was no Eden. People were always making that mistake; in letters, in discussions after he had read a few poems in public. 'That little green island was your Eden, of course' . . .

No. Even in infancy there are tears, rages, frustrations. The shadows that fell on him in school. The full sack at the end of a field that, someone had said, was 'poisonous' – a nameless dread that filled his mind. The blank terror, running away from another boy on the road between the school and the farm – a terror he only exorcised much later, writing a ballad about Achilles pursuing Hector under the wall of Troy. (Indeed, in the little island, everything assumed afterwards the dimension of epic, or of the archetypal biblical stories.)

Even then, in Wyre, aged five or six, he had knowledge of The Fall; he was in exile.

Time passed – the walls of the prison grew, they proliferated, they darkened, they threw up impassable new dead-ends just at the moment when he thought he had found a way out into the sun: in Kirkwall in his painful adolescence; in Glasgow when, twice a day, he had to pass through hideous slum-warrens going to and from his clerk's desk; in Europe (that continent of old-graces and sanctity and culture) that Hitler was soon to turn into a vast torture-chamber, slaughter-house, graveyard . . .

He trembled, remembering the deepening darkening ever-growing world-encompassing labyrinth. His heart quickened with pity and grief and anger.

The image of Eden saves us; without it we are lost and ruined, we ('a little lower than the angels') are worse than the beasts (who, however cruel and predatory, live in innocence, in their fifth day of creation); I am lost, the whole world is lost, sunk under the burden of a shameful history. Ruin. Eternal winter reigns.

> 'Yet still from Eden springs the root
> As clean as on the starting day.'

He paused. The back of the envelope was crammed with words, scored and scarred like a battlefield. Those biros were terrible, with their blue smudgings. His fingers were fouled with blue stains, dappled among the brown nicotine stains.

He had been this way before. Perhaps he should abandon the poem. It was good, thus far – it sang – but the music should open into something new and strange. Otherwise there might be justice in the sneer, 'Muir writes the same poem over and over.'

He found a sheet of paper with a few notes in it, slipped into a book he would be quoting from to his students: Marlowe's *Faustus*.

Below his window, in the Italian garden with its formal plots and beautiful octagonal sundial, and the River Esk and the beech-trees beyond, came the laughter of a few Newbattle students. He thought of Willa, his wife; with solicitude and love, long ago, Willa had saved his sanity, and very likely, his life; taking him by the hand out of that black maze into the sun and freedom. Now they were both unwell, in their different ways – she with crippling arthritis, he with vague ailments (heart and stomach) – and yet their love, after thirty years, was deeper and richer than ever. Willa's laughter could rouse the whole college like a struck bell.

A bird fluttered between the leaf-laden branches of a beech – a quick quiver and flutter and poise and fall – 'adventurous bird walking upon the air' . . . He had written that line once.

'The world is a pleasant place' – another line he had written, in his elegy for that young talented beautiful Orkney writer Ann Scott-Moncrieff, so tragically dead a few months after uttering these very words.

> *'The world is a pleasant place,*
> I can hear your voice repeat,
> When the sun shone on your face
> Last summer in Princes Street.'

It is not all a vale of tears, this life. Angels come, mysteriously, with jars of solace and refreshment and delight.

What place more beautiful than this old abbey, on a summer evening, with incenses of old gracious living, and yet older sanctity, in his nostrils, and Gavin at the piano in the drawing room, and the students drifting through the green maze of the garden below, laughing and chatting in a dozen different dialects; and the song birds, and the murmur of the river?

A spring of gratitude opened inside him. The words spilled on to the page. It was all that his leaky old biro could do to marshal them.

'But famished field and blackened tree
Bear flowers in Eden never known.
Blossoms of grief and charity
Bloom in these darkened fields alone.
What had Eden ever to say
Of hope and faith and pity and love
Until was buried all its day
And memory found its treasure trove?
Strange blessings never in Paradise
Fall from these beclouded skies.'

There! The poem was finished. The blood danced along his veins. The black prison door was thrown open. He was so exhausted with the joy, the achievement of the work – a new song in the world – that he had to lean back in the chair till his heart quieted a little . . . The first flush over, he would take it to Willa in the sitting-room of their flat and read it to her. And Willa would stroke his silver hair, smiling, and say, 'Weel done, peedie-breeks.'

Then they might have a glass of wine together.

And they would get out the map and discuss their so-much-looked-forward-to-holiday when the session was over.

No flying. Neither of them liked airplanes. It would have to be that car, Edwin driving all the way north through Scotland to Scrabster. He had never got used to cars and driving. Then the ferry-boat *St Ola* to the summer islands.

One day . . . one fine Orkney day . . . his imagination dazzled for a moment with the crystal of the vision . . . they would cross over on a little boat to Wyre – the island whose dust and streams and spindrift he was made of (with a breath of the eternal essence in it – who knows how?) – and they would stand together, hand in hand, beside a cornfield he had known in his angel-infancy . . .

3

Kolbein Hruga, Laird of Wyre island in Orkney, was in a towering rage.

The oatfield was ready for cutting, and half the harvesters were not there.

A dozen men had pushed the boats out after sunrise and rowed here and there, under the cliffs of Evie and Rousay to lift creels. They knew well enough that there would be a storm soon – maybe not today or tomorrow – but soon. They must save their creels and lobsters. They could feel the chill and stir of imminent tempest in their blood.

Kolbein Hruga felt the stir and growl and coldness in his bones too. A storm was coming! What was more important, a few lobsters or the corn harvest? If the gale brought rain with it, the whole harvest – blond saturated swirls – might be laid in ruins.

The ripe burnish had come on the crop suddenly, in the last day or two.

A few labourers whetted their sickles on the stones, lingering at the edge of the big field.

The great man raged here and there, indoors and out. The children hid round the corners of byre and barn and stye. The women moved mutedly about their tasks. Today it was the preparation of open-air harvest food: baskets of bannocks and cheese, gulls' eggs and cold rabbit, crocks of ale; for the cutters to refresh themselves at mid-day.

'The fools!' cried Kolbein in the door of the barn. 'They'll have to get out of this island! They can go where they like! They don't work for me any more . . . I say "field work" and what do they do, the scum? They push out the boats for a few scrawny lobsters!' . . .

Two or three of the younger women were white in the face. An old woman laughed: Kolbein's aunt. She had heard these rages and threats before, many a time.

Twenty sickles glittered in the sun that was too bright – the rain-breeding sun.

Kolbein's wife, Hilda, said mildly, 'You'll burst a blood vessel, man. The boats are coming back. Look, in Eynhallow Sound.'

There were the half-dozen truant boats, coming in fast on the tide. One man, Grot, stood in the bow of the leading boat and held two lobsters high; one in each hand – sign of a good catch.

'Well,' said Kolbein Hruga, 'but they shouldn't have gone without my leave.'

The waters round the little green island of Wyre gleamed and glittered and gloomed; unnaturally quiet: another sign of coming tempest.

Kolbein's rage had largely abated.

The fishermen came up from the shore.

Soon there were a score of sickles flashing and sussurating among the ripe oats.

'Lots of thistle and charlock in the oats this harvest,' said one old reaper.

It was always at times of crisis, like harvest or the eve of the Viking cruise, or during the assembly of the farmers at Tingwall, with the Earl present, that the rages of Kolbein Hruga were at their worst. That ferocious temper was famous all over the north and west. 'Kolbein the dragon,' men called him . . . 'Kolbein of Wyre'll get thee,' mothers would threaten ill-behaved children all over Orkney.

But most of the time Kolbein Hruga was a decent generous fair-minded man. Men were generally eager to serve in his ships and his fields. The famous rages died as suddenly as they were begotten. Then the laird of Wyre, for a while, would look ashamed and embarrassed. Sometimes he would row alone to the little monastery on Eynhallow, and let tranquillity come on him in the chapel there.

But at harvest time – especially on a harvest like this, so full of promise and of storm-menace – that temper was liable to blaze higher and longer than usual.

The thunders gathered head and broke out at mid-day, when the harvesters were eating and drinking under the stooks.

The farmer got to his feet suddenly, ale-froth in his whiskers, a hare-leg in his hand. 'Bjarni!' he yelled. 'That boy, where is he? Where is my son Bjarni? I told him to be here today, in the harvestfield . . . I made it plain to him before he went to bed. *You are to be in the oatfield tomorrow. If you're to be the farmer here, after I'm dead, you must learn everything about the farm – everything, from ploughing to threshing and winnowing. Yes, and horses and swine and bees, too – you must know all these things thoroughly. A fat lot of good all that dreaming will be, when you come to be laird of Wyre. Be in the harvest field first thing tomorrow – see to it . . .* That's what I told my son Bjarni last night . . . Where is he? I'll kill that boy! I'll thrash him within an inch of his life!' . . .

'Bjarni's young,' said his mother. 'There's plenty of time for him to learn.'

'You speak when you're spoken to!' cried Kolbein. 'The boy has disobeyed me. There's nothing more to be said.'

The sun shone with an unnatural pellucid brightness out of the sky that had not one cloud in it.

'Stop guzzling and gnawing!' shouted Kolbein to his harvesters. 'There's the barley-field to cut after this. The storm's not far off' . . .

The harvesters lined up with their sickles poised. 'That boy,' Kolbein was muttering still, 'I'll . . . I'll . . . I don't know what I'll do to him' . . .

There was one man in Wyre who did no useful work of any kind. His name was Arn. Twenty years ago, Arn had been bowman in Kolbein Hruga's longship in the Viking cruise to Man and Scilly. On a raiding foray into Angelsea, for food and drink, because their stores were low, Arn had been struck in the eye by a Welsh arrow. 'Oh,' cried he, 'on one side of me it's night, and sunny on the other side.' They had dragged him back, bleeding and half-dead, down the beach and on to the longship. At the same time they dragged a slaughtered pig and a dozen new cheeses out of a farm press. Welsh stones came bounding and bouncing and splashing after them. 'Push off,' cried Kolbein, 'before they stove in the hull.'

Arn, with his bleeding face, said that that had been a good day's work.

They plastered his eye with egg-yolk and herbs and bandaged it.

But it was noticed that, though he tried hard, Arn couldn't work on the *Otter* as well as he had done before.

One morning, off Cornwall, while they were having breakfast on board, they saw that Arn was groping to find his cup and plate. 'It's nothing,' said Arn. 'My eyes were such good mates, the good eye has kept grieving all the time for the lost eye. In the night the good eye went to join his brother. A good time to slip off, in the black night. They are both lost in this sunrise. And so, Kolbein, I'm blind from this day forward' . . .

After that, Arn seemed somewhat to regain his strength, and on the long voyage home he could row in deep water as well as the other oarsmen, once the oar was put in his hands. 'There are a lot of poor sights that I'm glad not to see any more,' said Arn. 'Ugly bad-tempered women. Weeds in a fine cornfield. Harps and hives made by bad workmen.'

Arn had always been a good reciter and story-teller. Now, whenever there was a lull on the voyage north, Arn would recite some of the old sagas and poems to them.

'I never heard you perform so well before, Arn,' said Kolbein the skipper, 'either at a wedding or a harvest-home or at Yule.'

'They put out the eyes of song-birds to make them sing better,' said Arn.

The upshot was that when *Otter* got home to Orkney, Kolbein Hruga gave Arn a little croft to live in, rent-free; and he saw to it that Arn never lacked for food and ale; and he commissioned a good craftsman in Trondheim to make a splendid harp for Arn the Eyeless.

The blind poet Arn was once more instructing the boy Bjarni Kolbeinson in the craft of verse-making. It was such a sultry afternoon that even inside Arn's croft they could hear the sickles cutting crisply into the corn, and the reapers calling to each other, and the pure spillings of a lark high above in the blue sky.

'A poem must ring like a breastplate or a helmet,' said Arn. 'There's no craft so like the skald's as the smith at his forge and anvil. The fire is blown to a white heat, the hammer rings, the poem is welded together, line after line, with strong consonants, and at last the poem lies there on the bench, a thing of cold power and beauty. That's to say, of course, if the word-smith knows his craft.'

'I want to be a poet,' said the boy.

'You're not the first one to have said that. Let me tell you, it is not so easy. It will take all your strength and courage. A

good inspiration might strike you. Words come, well ordered, the fluent vowels, the strong consonants binding the
poem together. All seems to be well. And then . . . And then,
just when the end seems to be in sight, just when it is time to
deliver the final hammer-stroke, something goes wrong, the
poem falls to pieces in your hands. Or you know, beyond a
doubt, the shape of it is wrong. Reluctantly, you throw it on
the scrap-heap.'

'I will endure disappointments,' said Bjarni. 'I'm prepared
for that.'

They heard, from the distant part of Wyre, a voice. 'Where
is that boy? I'll thrash him black and blue.'

'The father,' said Arn. 'Kolbein is angry. That too you will
have to endure if you want to be a skald. Anger, impatience,
contempt. Life is real. Life is earnest. They stamp their feet,
these men of action. *There are real things to be done. That
word-juggling is all right, beside a winter fire with an ale-horn.
Not at harvest-time. Not when there's a longship to be launched
for a cruise* . . . You'll have to learn to put up with such
ignorant talk. Without our poems, their voyages and their
sieges are a dance of shadows.'

Then again, far off, 'Bjarni! Bjarni!' came on the sultry air.
And a few of the women cried with sweet voices, 'Bjarni!'

'Oh,' said the lost boy. 'I *will* be a poet! . . . Nothing will
stop me. I want to make poems about everything. The whole
world is so beautiful. Listen to the lark! Look to the lark!
Look at the heavy bronze of the barley stalks. There's a girl
down there binding sheaves with her sisters. Biorg. Why does
my heart miss a beat when I look at Biorg? Last winter I could
look at Biorg quite coldly – she meant nothing to me. Now
since midsummer all I want to do is make songs for Biorg.
Am I in love, Arn? Is that it? I will – no matter how difficult it
is – make a great love-poem for Biorg the corngatherer.'

'Bjarni,' said the skald, 'I think I have been wasting my time with you. Verse is not for praising girls or skylarks or cornstalks. Verse is for putting courage and strength into a man. Surely, by this time, you understand that. Life is very short, a few breaths, a few heartbeats. So a man ought to pack into his short time as much action and danger as he can. Who wants to shrivel and gasp his few last breaths in a bed, aged a hundred? That's why the young men go into the thick of the fighting, under a castle in Ulster, or when the longships rear against each other off Cape Wrath. What is recorded about a warrior and his behaviour then – that is of supreme importance. What if he was to turn and run from axe and horseman? The last years of his life would be misery. He would be a reproach and a disgrace. No one would welcome such a man to their fire and table. The remnant of his days would be unendurable. The children mocking him, calling "coward" after him. It would be as if chisel and hammer had been taken to the lintel-stone of his house, and a shameful rune cut there. No, Bjarni, worse – for after he was dead the ghost of the coward would have no peace. It would go, shunned and pitiful among the shades, while his companions who behaved well that day, and died, sit at the feast-boards of Valhalla. Forever young and happy they are, the heroes, their after-life comforted with songs and mead and comradeship. Do they droop, sometimes, thinking of their ships and horses and women that they had to leave so soon? There is no sadness, they remember their courage and strength, especially if the tide of battle or siege was setting against them. "Courage shall be mightier as our strength lessens" . . . The praise of the poets is more pleasant than the meadbarrel. They have had their lives rounded with magnificent last words.'

'I think,' said Bjarni, 'I hear Biorg in the field now. It *is* Biorg! I must leave you now, Arn. Thank you for your lesson.

I must go now and join Biorg in the cornfield. But what can I say to her? I stand there, tongue-tied, whenever the stable-man's daughter is near.'

'Of course,' said Arn, 'the vikings don't all make wonderful spoken epitaphs for themselves, though to read the sagas you would think they did. No, boy, it is we poets and story-tellers who put the brave words into their mouths, and so worthily seal their lives, their deaths. I tell you, it is no easy thing to make a great last speech with a spear in your guts, or half your jaw sliced away by an axe.'

'I think I hear the monastery bell on Eynhallow,' said Bjarni. 'Listen. Is it Evensong?'

'So then the question arises,' said Arn. 'Is poetry sham and deceit? Is poetry lies? There will always be men to cast doubts on the worth of our craft. The word transfigures all. How should I put it? . . . The craft of poetry gathers all worthwhile events – voyages, battles, settlements – into one event, "the voyage", "the battle", "the settlement". Those scattered events are always in the end shadows and ashes, however much men try to convince themselves that they have come face to face with "real life". They go home with a sour taste in the mouth. They have missed the *meaning* of what happened . . . Then it is winter, time for ale-cups and harps. When the skald chants "voyage", all the voyages that ever were or ever will be are gathered into the one word. What he sings is "*the* battle", "*the* settlement". All the impurities, disappointments, dissatisfactions, are burned and hammered out. What remains is the pure symbol. The bronze helmet lies there, taken from the forge, well-made. Here is the meaning. The poet has given it to us. Men experience in verse the essence of their actions. They draw endless delight and courage from what they hear . . . Are you listening, boy?'

But Arn the poet had known for some time that a breath and a heart-beat were absent from his hearth.

Bjarni went round the shore towards the boat-noust.

The oatfield was all cut. The three-fold sheaves leaned together, rank after rank.

The harvesters had gone home. Here and there a lamp shone through an open door. The sun was down over Rousay, leaving a cloudless afterglow. The only man left in the harvest-field was the boy's father, Kolbein. Anxiously the farmer scanned the horizon. He licked his finger and held it high, seeking for a wind-airt. A westerly might mean rain. There was no wind. The evening was utterly still. The boy could hear a dog barking in Rousay – the plash of an oar off Egilsay.

He lingered, looking at one little croft. The shadow of a girl carrying a jar moved between the lamp and the door: Biorg. His heart missed a beat, then gave out a cluster of pulsings, for pure joy.

Ah, he must be careful not to cause a clatter among the flat shore stones! For then his father would know where he was. There would be a blaze of rage for sure in the twilight: enough to startle three or four islands around.

Instead, as the boy stood on a rock, under the sea-banks, a deeper stillness moved upon the silence. The monks were singing their office in the little monastery of Eynhallow. 'The peace that passeth understanding' – the phrase drifted through the boy's mind, as a perfect description of the plainchant.

Bjarni knew the monks and their way of life well. In Eynhallow he had gone to be educated for three winters.

It was only on a rare evening like this that the Eynhallow choir could be heard in Wyre.

He would be a poet. However his father might rage, he would be a poet in the north; his fame would go echoing here and there about the wide Scandinavian circle: Norway, Iceland, Faroe, Orkney and Shetland, Sutherland, the Hebrides, Man, Ireland. He would devote himself to the difficult craft until he had mastered it. Many years it might take. At last Bjarni would enrich the grey air of the north with poems. Not bronze: he would strive for a greater richness.

The sea moved, with pure murmurs, over the stones. The tide was rising. The sound of Eynhallow gleamed and gloomed. Bjarni could see a merchant ship on the horizon, beyond Rousay, drifting west. There was not enough wind for a sail. Now and then he heard a languid splash of oars. The sailors were in no hurry. Tonight they would have a clear star-chart to navigate by.

Now there was silence on Eynhallow. Bjarni listened. There was one little bell-cry. A line of shadows, bearing candles, moved into the chapel.

'Bjarni!' His father's rasping voice cut into the seamless silence. 'Bjarni! It's all right. Come home. So long as you help in the barleyfield in the morning. The rains will come sometime tomorrow, I'm sure of it.'

Well, if little Biorg of the honey-coloured hair and the blue eyes was to be in the harvest-field, he might go there with his sickle. Bjarni didn't mind farm work at all. But if Biorg was to be there, the reaping would be pure joy.

He wasn't ready yet though to face his father. He expected one blow at least, in spite of the words of truce – a wallop that would leave one side of his head numb and trilling for most of the morning.

Arn – Arn was one of those poets in the old mode: nothing counted but valour and blood and defiance; all the greed and cruelty of men held still and heraldic by a strict ordering of words. Bjarni had studied those poems all summer. He had admired the intricate craftsmanship. The tumult and the shouting too – they had stirred his blood more than a little. But the images were stale. The Nordic harp was too primitive for the new quickening that was abroad everywhere in Europe.

Stone clashed against stone under the boy's feet. He stopped, listening to the hammering of his heart. Silence. His father must have gone indoors for supper. Bjarni lingered. He leapt over a low reef. He came to the noust and the dozen fishing boats.

The star Hesper was out, brilliant in the west. It glittered across the brimming sea.

There, to the north, rose the dark tower of St Magnus church in Egilsay.

That old mode of poetry was withering. The crusading Vikings had brought new kinds of verse back with them from France and Italy. Poems of love and religious devotion and nature and romance, utterly different from the harsh boreal verse-forms that had come down from the past. In this new poetry the vowel was mistress, the consonant her devoted servant and squire. Fresh as flowers, as birds, as morning were those new lyrics out of France, and each poem exquisitely ordered into stanzas of intricate and various pattern, and the end of many lines chiming with like sounds, called rhyme. This new Mediterranean poetry was like spring taking over from winter. Hadn't Rognvald Kolson, the great Orkney earl and poet, nephew of Magnus the saint, experienced the new poetry on his great expedition to Rome and Jerusalem and Byzantium, only a generation before; especially in the court of Ermengarde, Countess of Narbonne, where he had lingered for a whole winter, enchanted with love and longing? Earl Rognvald had managed to tear himself at last out of the web. But as his fifteen ships drove east towards the sacred places Rognvald's mouth had brimmed over with poems to the young French widow Ermengarde – fine accomplished verses – but Rognvald Kolson had had to graft those new experiences on to the coarse stem of Scandinavian prosody, and the tree had put forth but a few scattered scentless blossoms.

> 'Your hair, lady
> Is long, a bright waterfall.
> You move through the warriors
> Rich and tall as starlight.
> What can I give
> For the cup and kisses brought to my mouth?
> Nothing.
> This red hand, a death-dealer.'

and

> 'The summer mouth of Ermengarde
> Commands two things –
> A sea of saga-stuff, wreckage, gold
> As far as Jordan,
> And later, at leaf-fall,
> On patched homing wings
> A sun-dark hero.'

By now Bjarni was afloat in one of the fishing boats. Instead of his father's curragh, Bjarni had chosen the boat *Scallop* that belonged to Biorg's father. To think that the girl had sometimes sat in the stern, trailing her lovely fingers in the sea! He rowed until the boat entered the tide-race, then boat and boy were borne west on the urgent darkling stream.

'Bjarni!' came a cry from the shore he had just left. His father was abroad, and vigilant, and enraged. 'Who told you you could take that boat? I'll break every bone in your body!'

The boy looked back once. Then he drove the steering oar into the tide-race and the boat plunged and snorted foam and they were free of the strong dark rasping ropes of the roost, and drifting calmly right under the wall of the monastery of Eynhallow.

Deeper and more pure than the waters came the plain-chant. Bjarni leaned out of the boat, listening. What psalm were they singing? He was beginning to forget the Latin, but once he recognized a phrase or two, the rest of the text came easily to his tongue, in his own Norn:

'When the Lord brought back the captives of Sion, we were like men dreaming.

Then our mouth was filled with laughter and our tongue with rejoicing.

Then they said among the nations, "The Lord has done great things for them".

The Lord has done great things for us; we are glad indeed.

Restore our fortunes, O Lord, like the torrents in the southern desert.

Those that sow in tears shall reap rejoicing.

Although they go forth weeping, carrying the seed to be sown,

They shall come back rejoicing, carrying their sheaves.'

Then there was silence in the monastery. Through the transept window the candle-flames fluttered like golden moths. There was a whispering and a rustle, like wind in corn. The monks had risen to their feet to hear the Gospel.

Bjarni recognized the voice of Father Anselm, who had said to him so earnestly on his very last day, after he had rolled up the Greek scroll and tied it with string, 'Bjarni, you have been our very best pupil here in Eynhallow. I know you have the vocation. You feel the truth and beauty of our way of life, don't you? Would you not consider a deeper study of theology, eh, in Oxford maybe, or Paris? I know it will not be easy, your father – God bless him – being the kind of man he is. If you like, Bjarni, I'd have a word with Kolbein Hruga myself . . . We can teach you no more here, in Eynhallow. Go in peace.'

Whether the abbot had actually spoken to the laird of Wyre, concerning Bjarni's religious vocation, the boy didn't know. But no more was ever heard of it. Very likely, if they had met and spoken, Kolbein Hruga had sent the abbot away with a bee in his ear. That was two summers ago now. In the meantime, Fate had taken a hand in the game. Bjarni Kolbeinson would be a poet, not a priest.

Yet he remembered always, with joy, Eynhallow and the monks.

Father Anselm was reading the Gospel.

. ∴ . 'The kingdom of heaven is likened unto a man which sowed good seed in his field . . .'

Laus tibi, Christe, murmured the brothers, and sat down with a rustle of skirts.

Bjarni turned the boat *Scallop* round. It would be hard, rowing back against the tide.

It would be harder still, having beached the boat, to go home and have his father rise from the fireside bench to face him. What would the boy say? 'Father, I have made up my mind. I am going to devote my life to poetry . . .' He wasn't brave enough for that. If he spoke with a certain degree of humility in his voice, before the old man could rise up from his bench, 'Father, I'm sorry I wasn't at the oatfield today. I couldn't get away from Arn and that harp of his. I was stuck like a fly in honey. I just rowed out a little, it was such a beautiful evening. Father, I'll be out in the barley-field first thing in the morning. Sooner than the lark.'

He dipped his oars in the Sound. He rose up from the thwart to drive the blades through the contrary murmurous waters. The plainchant faded. He could see, from mid-Sound, that the Eynhallow barley-field was already cut. How tired the monks must be!

The islands glittered, low dark emeralds, all around.

The Christmas Dove

The rich merchant had a house on the hill outside the town. Servants came and went in the rooms, and tended the stable and garden and wells.

The merchant's children fed a dove in a golden cage, on cake and sweetmeats.

One day the smallest child left the cage door open, and the bird was up and away into the wind and sun. A servant tried to catch it, but it flew from his fingers and the servant measured his length in the dust.

Tearfully the children trooped into their father's office, to tell him about the lost dove.

'Tut-tut,' said he. 'Go away – I'm busy. Can't you see the clerks writing in the account books – a camel train leaves for Syria tomorrow. I've told you a hundred times not to come to the office during business hours . . . Sammy, tears is it? Why are you crying? The dove flown away – is that all? I'll buy three doves at the market tomorrow. Now go and leave us to get on with our work . . . Sixty bales of wool. A hundred jars of best oil . . .'

The merchant's children came out into the yard with dark stains on their faces.

There they saw a servant who was dust from head to foot, and with scratches on his arms. (This was the servant who had tried to catch the dove.) The children pointed at him. They laughed.

The dove was frightened. It had lived its whole life in the cage, from the time of the breaking of the egg, and the yellow wind and the stone alleys and the people coming and going in the village frightened it. The town birds darted at it. One bird cried: 'What are you, fluttering stranger?' And another with dusty wings said: 'Fly away, you milksop, there's little enough bread and seeds in this town . . .' A red bird screamed: 'Look out for the hawk! He lives up there, high, in his crystal cage of wind.'

Dearly the dove would have loved to be back in his safe golden cage in the merchant's villa, with children feeding him cherries and sweet crusts. But he did not know the way.

The dove flew out of the town, with its noise, dust and hostility. He darted over the desert sand, blown into undulations by the wind, with its palm trees and oases of water, and the golden eye of the sun above. Suddenly the sun was fractured, a wavering shadow covered the dove, and when he looked up what he saw was the yellow eye of the hawk.

The dove almost fell from the air, he was so frightened! But he gathered what wits and courage he had left, and he turned and flew towards a little green hill with sheep grazing on it, and a shepherd boy with a long crook. The dove fell panting on a stone. The sheep looked at him mildly. The boy broke off a piece of his loaf and offered it to him. Then the boy went down to the stream with a cup and filled it for the lost bird. The dove had never tasted anything as delicious as the oaten crust and the broken circles in the cup of water.

When the dove looked up, he could see the hawk going in a slow dark wheel northwards, after other prey.

'What's that boy up to now?' he heard a dark grumbling voice say. 'Look, boy, we don't keep you to feed a useless bird, we keep you to see that the sheep are safe. There's a ewe over there that's put her hoof in a bunch of thistles. See to it . . .'

Three shepherds came up from the village, each with a skin of wine, and all they did was complain about the village inn and the hordes of strangers in the village, and how the innkeeper was taking advantage of the situation to put up the price of his wine again. 'The scoundrel!' . . . 'An outrage.'

The boy ran to take the prickles out of the ewe's leg. The dove, frightened by the shepherds, unfurled his grey pinions to fly away. 'A good sign, a dove,' said one of the shepherds. 'It's usually that hawk after a new lamb.'

The dove scattered grey blessings on the sheep-fold, and flew south, away from the vigilant hawk. Now the sun had moved down the sky, and as it touched the horizon a flush engulfed the desert. Through an air red as wine the dove spied, far below, three travellers with laden camels. The travellers halted. They unburdened the camels and tethered them. They lit a fire under a rock. One opened a bag and passed food – oranges and cakes – to his companions. A silver wine flask shone in the firelight, passing from hand to hand, from mouth to mouth.

This too was a scene of peace. The dove trembled in the darkening air, then faltered and fell on the rock near the little tableau of travellers and animals, fire and refreshment.

'A dove!' cried one of the men. 'When it hung up there trembling, I thought it was our sign again.'

'Welcome, bird of peace,' said a deep gentle black voice. He offered a date to the dove. The dove took it into his beak.

'Fly away, dove,' said the third man. 'The desert is a dangerous place for you to be. Aren't you afraid of the hawk? There'll be nothing left of you after sunrise if you don't find a lodging, nothing but a few bones in the sand.'

'The whole world is a dangerous place,' said the traveller

whose voice was like a golden harp. 'The meaning of history will be Death, all time will be a scattering of bones, unless we find the place soon.'

The dove flew higher and higher up among the stars. He hung there, trembling, uncertain which way to turn. Then, over the desert, he saw far away the lights of the little town. That was where he belonged. There were the children and the golden cage and the circles of cake and milk and safety.

But where, in all that hundred houses great and small, was the house he belonged to?

The dove hovered over the darkling town, with its watchman's lantern at the main gate, and the lamps burning in prosperous windows, and candles in poor men's niches.

The dove was as lost as he had been all day. (And somewhere the hawk sat furled, nourishing himself with dreams of blood and death.)

The dove, stooping lower, saw a friend! The shepherd boy, with a small lamb in his arms, had entered the town gate and now had set his face to the darkest part of the town. The dove hovered above the boy and the lamb. 'I'll come to no harm,' said the dove to himself, 'if I stay near this boy.'

The boy stooped in at a dark door, where there was only a glim of light. Shadowy animals moved about inside. It was (thought the dove) the poorest house in the town. A tall shadow, a man, bent over a kneeling shadow that held a bundle in her arms.

The shepherd boy stood in the doorway, afraid to go in.

But the dove flew on to the boy's shoulder, and paused there a moment, and flew up to a cold rafter, and furled there, under the stars.

The Stone Rose

The little kings of Pictland sent bands of men against each other: a few died on the moors and in the lochs.

Or a raiding party went out at night, in summer, and came back at dawn driving a few cattle or sheep.

At those times, songs would be made. A man would strike the harp after sunset and his voice would sink and soar, celebrating a great victory. Then the harper would remember the dead bodies in the heather; his voice keened with lamentation and loss. The people felt purified by those chants. The elegies too filled them with wonderment.

What laughter, when the harper sang about the night-raiders: how cunning they were, driving the bullocks away from the edge of the pastoral village on the other side of the mountain, while the villagers slept . . .

A dawn wind rose, and blew the songs away like petals. A phrase or an image here and there was remembered, sometimes a whole chant if the harper chanced to be a good man at his craft. And sometimes, if the song was very good, it might linger among the people for a generation or two, after the harper was dead. But it was never repeated exactly like the first singing – words and names were forgotten, a rhythm was altered, an image blurred or changed (and sometimes it changed for the better, if there happened to be a young poet of talent in the tribe.)

*   *   *

They were not always fighting or stealing, the tribes of Pictland. Sometimes they traded with each other. They would agree to meet at the mountain pass, or on the shore of a loch. Bargaining went on all day. 'We will give you so much of this salmon – and good sweet firm fresh salmon they are – touch them. Now, what will you offer in return?'

The bargainer – usually the man with the most plausible tongue in the village – would be answered by another subtle mouth. 'Here are hides of the very finest quality – such suppleness, such strength! But there will need to be many more salmon before we part with such excellent hides.'

So the wrangling went on, half in earnest and half in jest, all morning.

'And we have a few surplus ponies – offspring of the wind, yet strong as the earth itself – that we could let you have, if you have something of quality to give us in exchange . . .'

'Fergus has made too many skin boats this summer – they are so swift and beautiful we hate to part with them – look at them – look at the curve of the oars! They skim the sea like birds. There should be many ponies for a boat like that' . . .

So it went on all day. And the people of both villages came to the bargaining place. There was much enjoyment in the haggling: it was more like a game than the serious business of life, for the survival of the people through the tempests and snows of winter depended on having adequate supplies of all kinds. The harpers came to the markets, and there were dancing and dalliance and teasing and gift-giving.

At last, by nightfall, the exchange was made: so many salmon for so many hides, so many ponies for the ox-hide boat with oars and mast.

But no party was ever entirely satisfied. Each village went home, pleased with the day's merry-making, but sure that somehow or other they had been cheated, outwitted, done down . . .

Harvest came, and the first cold winds, and the stars, and snow.

Then it was time for the young men to form the first raiding-party of the winter. This was an activity more primitive and heroic and worthy of harp-songs than bargaining at the mountain pass.

One midnight the raiders carried home one of their group who had fallen on ice and broken his leg. The byres were locked fast, they said, the sheep-fold was guarded. They took nothing home but their injured comrade.

The harp was silent for a night or two.

The villagers said nothing. They knew it would have been better if the young man had been left in the snow to die. From now on, till old age and death, he would be only a burden to the tribe. He could not hunt or fish or plough or fight. In a bad winter, it was hard enough for the strong villagers to come through alive to the time of ox and plough; the old and feeble ones, and the young sickly children, most of them died in the black heart of winter.

So they left the young man with the twisted leg in a cave. His friends came with kindling and food and drink. *Bring me pieces of sharp flint*, said the useless one. So they brought him a bag of sharp flint-stones. With the flint-stones the man scratched pictures on the wall of his cave – a wild boar, a harp, a fishing boat, an eagle, a hunter, a ship (but they knew only small boats like cormorants – never a great black swan like this).

Nothing like pictures had been seen before on the mountain. The elders came to look at the pictures in the firelight. A few could see only a few meaningless scratches. Others saw the fleetingness of their days made into a kind of ceremony, a dance without music.

Between the hunter and the boar, while the elders probed
the wall with their eyes, the cripple one scratched an arrow.
Then was seen what had not been seen before: that the bow
of the hunter was slack, and the throat of the wild boar was
open to the arrow.

They laughed. They shook their heads in wonderment.

A few quick strokes, some up, some down, made a mesh:
and the fish on the wall of the cave was tumbling and curling
into it.

An old man pointed to the big ship. 'What is that?' he said.
'I have not seen a boat like that before.'

Nor had the others. The scratcher-on-stone did not know
what the shape was, either.

'My hand was compelled to it,' he said, 'as surely as it was
compelled, in the time of my comeliness, to touch the face of
a girl.'

A few young men said, the following summer, that there
had never been such good pig-hunting or cod-fishing that
they could remember. There must be a magic in the stone
scratchings.

Others said no – that was chance, some summers were
bounteous, others stingy: the figures on the cave wall had
nothing to do with it.

But here, now, in this cave, one night of winter's beginning, while the village men peered at the pictures, in
incomprehension or wonder, an outcry was heard from
the houses below. Women were screaming and howling
with rage.

There had been a raid from the men on the other side of
the mountain – twenty cattle were missing, the sheep-fold
was empty, the chief's house was burning! It looked like
being a bad winter for the tribe.

The only unconcerned one was the cripple artist. In the

Celtic tongue they called him 'he-who-makes-things-and-events-into-silent-music'.

What few remnants there were to eat that winter, a girl brought up to him. And she brought him a sheepskin to keep him warm. And she carried logs in her apron for his fire. Fortunately, after the solstice, there were some good hauls of cod.

Time passed. The old ones died, children were born, there were feuds and skirmishes and harp-songs in winter; in summer hunting and trading, and the anxious vigil over the corn-patches.

The village men who bargained at the mountain pass or by the loch-side had learned a few things from the cripple artist in the cave. Trading was no longer a random crude exchange. For the village men came to the market place not only with their produce: skin-boats and well-made wooden benches and smoked rolls of ham, but with an inventory drawn on sheepskin with a stick charred in the fire – exact numbers of each item of exchange.

There was resistance to such cold calculation – it took all the fun and merriment out of bargaining, said this one and that – but in the course of a few winters all the villages in the west of Alba carried to the markets, along with their produce, the inventory. But no inventory was so well and truly drawn as the one made by the cripple artist, with its symbols of boar and honeycomb and boat and the exact number opposite each, in parallel strokes.

Always there was a concourse of people – dancing and drinking and harping round the few booths in the market-place. Those who had thieved and pillaged from each other in the winter met and exchanged news and drank with each other on the market-day. Little gifts were given and exchanged. Young men and women from different villages, occasionally, looked at each other with enchanted eyes. (But this was frowned upon by the elders: the web of kinship should never be sullied by an alien strand; even though all the peoples for hundreds of miles around were Picts and spoke the same language and sent up rich smoke to the same gods.)

And always, the girl who tended his fires brought from the market a little gift to 'him-who-makes-things-and-creatures-and-events-into-silent-music' – a cairngorm, it could be, or a fresh-water pearl, or the skin of a hare to keep the cold out of his fingers next winter.

Rumours came to the Pictish tribes of the west. Sea-dragons had appeared in the northern seas; the dragons spewed men out of their bellies, and those men swarmed over the island shores, burning and destroying and plundering and killing.

What were those dragons? Who were these sons of the dragon and where did they come from? Would they come at last to the islands and sea-lochs of the west?

Some said there was no truth in the rumours. They were stories made at the winter fires in the north to frighten women and children . . .

Alba was full of wanderers at that time – men who went here and there, and brought scraps of news in exchange for a bite and a night's sleep beside the fire.

Some of the wanderers spoke of the terrible dragon-men. Now, they said, the dragon-men did not simply come out of the east and burn and plunder and go away again. They drove the people out of their little farms and bothies and took possession of them. Only the best land: the men in the dragons were interested only in the best land: let the Pictish farm-folk do what they could with bog and heather and moor. Some of the invaders brought their own women from the east; others took the loveliest and the strongest Pictish girls to be their wives.

'The wandering ones are liars,' said the chief elder. 'They are and they always have been liars and scare-mongers and seers of ghosts.'

But the children demanded to hear more about the sea-dragons and the dragon-men who were there, suddenly, out of the sun-rise, striking at an island shore; the mouths with the terrible songs in them; the axes flashing in the first light.

'God forbid the dragon-men come here!' cried an old woman.

One day in winter one of those travelling tale-bearers happened to visit the cave where the cripple artist lived. The eyes of the man were so used to living things – to creatures in all the tremulous delicate motions of life, and in the great purposeful leaps and surges of stag and eagle and whale – that he did not recognize the scratched fish and pig and eagle. To him they were only a confusion of lines and curves. But suddenly he stopped before the drawing of 'the ship' – he drew back as if he had been slapped across the face, or as if a bucket of cold water had been poured over him. 'That's it,' he cried. 'That's the dragon-ship! That's how I saw it anchored in a bay in Orkney. How is it possible to make such magic with a few lines? And what's more – such a ship has never been seen near this coast! How could *you* know this, a cripple man, a scratcher with stone upon stone?'

In the village they boiled a bit of fish for the wanderer's breakfast and sent him on his way. He intended travelling into Ireland, he told them.

Another wandering man came. 'The foreigners from the east,' he said, 'are now well established in Orkney. They have settled down, they are farmers. There are still a few danger-ous dragon-ships. But mostly the sailors want to barter and trade in the lands of the Saxons, and further, in the places called France and Sicily'.

A wanderer came one winter. A dragon-ship had been wrecked on the island called Barra – smashed to pieces on the rocks. The islanders did not go near the ship for days. A few bodies were found, scattered on other shores. The Barra men had managed to salvage one unbreached barrel from the wreck; the staves of other barrels were strewn everywhere. Two or three of the younger men tasted the drink in the barrel – it was not at all like their ale and usquebaugh. Soon all the Barra men were clustered about the barrel, lapping the red drink out of their cupped hands. There had never been such a night in the island of Barra – dancing, singing, fighting. 'The drink has more of the sun in it than our bleak malt,' an old Barra man had said next morning . . . And yes, true enough, the prow of the broken ship was a dragon, all black and red, terrible to behold . . . So the wandering man reported.

In the last two or three years, the cripple man in the cave had gone on working. But now he seemed to be no longer so interested in drawing fish and deer and hawks and hunters. 'I will simplify the drawings,' he said to the girl who lit his fires and brought him cheese and bread. 'They will be clearer and more meaningful from now on. This silent music on the wall – it will say delicate and subtle things by means of a few strokes. Is it necessary to draw the eye and the gill and the scales of a fish? No, a simple outline is enough, one stroke with a sharp edge on the wall, and all men – at least, those with the wit to see it – say, "fish". In the same way, a cunning curve or two, and there is a hawk butting into the wind. Alter a curve, there is the hawk, poised. Another arc, narrower, down-tilted – the hawk has fallen! Similarly with a man: the man can be at the same time simplified and made subtle in the drawing, so that he who looks will say at once, "he is a lover", "he is a thief", "he is a man who likes the sea better than the mountain", "he is a coward", "he is a good warrior" . . .'

'Your porridge is getting cold,' said the girl.

But the cripple man was beyond hunger. 'Now,' he said, 'if it were possible to arrive at a final simplicity, so that the silent music on the wall becomes one with the music of our speech, that would be a great marvel, wouldn't it? I am abroad on an ocean of meaning – I don't know where it will take me, this speculation about sign and speech, but I think it will be impossible for me even to reach the far shore.'

'You must eat,' said the girl, 'or you'll die, that's all I know.'

Suddenly, one morning when the village woke, it was out there in the sea loch, anchored: a ship. The wooden prow of the ship glared at them, all red and black, a dragon!

The sight shook the children out of the honey of sleep – they peered, sticky-eyed, at the wonder, lingering at the loch shore. But the women were already packing. Cheeses and sacks of meal and spinning-wheels they were piling together at the end of the village, ready for the flight into the mountains. The men were rounding up the goats and cattle and pigs. There was no time to lose! They knew the secret valleys where no sea-raiders could find them or their herds. The harper was there with his harp slung at his shoulder. The old folk were given light things to carry, cheese-moulds and horn spoons and partan-creels.

The backs of the men bristled with arrows. Long spears lay aslant in their arms. It might come to a battle in the mouth of the pass, higher up.

There was as yet no stir of life on the dragon-ship. The silence was worse to endure than rage and shouting.

'They will burn my house,' said a young woman with a baby in her arms. 'The house my man built in April.'

'Everything is ready,' said the man called 'hunter-of-stags'. 'It is time for us to take to the corries and the clefts.'

The man who was the chief elder in the village had done nothing since sunrise but stand at the shore and shade his eyes towards the ship anchored in the loch.

'I think we will stay awhile,' he said.

The women shrieked against him.

'Let the women go,' said the old man. 'Let them take the children and the beasts and the looms. Let the old ones go with them. Something is happening on this coast that has never happened before. I didn't think I would live to see such a thing. Who knows what might come out of a day that has begun so strangely? Let the women go. It will be good to be rid of the noise and clatter of them for a while.'

The women set out up one of the mountain paths, with children running before and old ones trailing behind. Sheep surged before them in a tremulous mass.

'Grip your weapons tight,' said the chief. 'If it comes to a fight, we will fight them on this shore. The sea loch has cradled and kept us since the time of the stories. The dust of the old dead ones should not be disturbed by foreigners.'

There stood then on the shore with the old chief all the men of the village, some with spears, some with arrows, and one boy who was so skilful with the sling that last winter he had brought down a hawk.

The harper was there. It was noticed that he was trembling. He looked often up at the mountain cave where a young woman was standing.

'Go to the caves,' said the chief to the harper. 'You would be better there, indeed.'

Still the harper stayed.

'Let him play his harp,' said the smith. 'That might frighten the dragon-men away.'

They laughed along the shore of the loch.

Then they heard a slithering and clashing of loose stones. The maker of pictures came and stood beside them, and the young woman who looked after him always, in spite of jeers and insults.

'Here are two more nuisances,' said the chief. 'They would be better on the mountainside too.'

The sun took a golden step through the sky.

The tide began to turn. The loch water surged gently among the feet of the village men.

The artist lifted a smooth round pebble from the shore. He began to make markings on it with his hard flint-edge.

'Is this a time to be making pictures?' said the chief. 'We might all be dead before the sun goes down' . . .

The artist sketched on the pebble a little scatter of houses and a ship and a dove flying between.

Now the village could see a face at the helm. Other faces appeared at the ship's side. The black-bearded villagers thought it strange that the hair of the foreigners was bright like honey. But their faces were gaunt and dark with southern suns.

The artist said to the boy with the sling, 'Will you send this stone into the ship?'

'I'll try,' said the boy.

The stone flew from shore to ship like a bird.

'They won't like that,' said the chief. 'This will bring them out like bees from a hive.'

The villagers could see how the shipmen were passing the stone from hand to hand to hand.

'It was a message of peace,' said the harper. 'I could read that much.'

Already the artist was scratching another pebble. He drew a few small boats, a net, fishes.

The rising tide washed among the ankles of the men.

'They will understand these pictures,' said the harper. 'We are simple fishing folk. The sea in the west is ours from ancient times. This peace should not be broken.'

The stone flew from the sling and bounced about in the ship.

A dozen bright heads bent over the stone.

The ship returned no answer.

'You are wasting your time,' said the chief. 'I think the dragon-men are trying to wear us out with delay and dread . . . You, girl, go up to the caves. This is no place for women.'

The artist was putting scratches on another smooth pebble. 'Let her stay,' he said. 'She is often a nuisance, but let her stay.'

The harper looked at the marks on the stone: curve of plough, crowned cornstalk, ox-horns. He said, 'They will understand the writing. This people do not gnaw brutish bones. This folk are friends of the sun, friends of the plough-scrolled earth. The men of this coast have a treaty with beast and sun and bread . . . That's what the stone says.'

The stone dropped into the ship like a bird.

The loch water, bright and brimming, washed about their knees. The villagers did not seem to notice.

The sailors studied this third stone for a long time. Fingers went here and there on the script. Heads nodded. The helmsman seemed to smile, a dazzle of teeth in the tarnish of his beard.

'I have seen smiles before,' said the chief. 'The wild-cat smiles before he sinks his teeth in.'

The artist was busy at another smooth round stone. Ovals and circles and curves only, in three piles on one side of the stone, and balancing all on the other side of the stone a huge circle like the sun.

The harper shook his head over those marks.

'I hope,' said the artist, 'that the dragon-men are not as ignorant as you.'

'Now I see it,' cried the harper suddenly. 'In one of the circles I see the water of our well, trembling. In other circles I see the light loaves our women bake and their heavy cheeses. The ovals are eggs from the cliff. The curves are ox-ribs. The great circle – let me see – the big circle is the gift they will give for our gifts, a golden ring maybe.'

'Deliver the message well,' said the artist to the boy. The sling made five circles in the air and the stone flew from it and one of the men in the ship ducked his head to avoid being struck.

The helmsman examined the stone first. Then he passed it to the sailors. They discussed it while the sun took another step through the sky.

The helmsman waved his hand across the water to the villagers.

'Now,' said the elder, 'grip your spears well. No, the arrows first, then the spears. For I think we are going to be invaded.'

It was only one sailor who leapt from the ship into the cold loch water. The head sank and surfaced, and flung water about.

A face flashed across the loch, in a burst of sunlight, there at the flood's height.

A hand held high a square of wood, with knife-marks scored on it, white and new. Then with powerful strokes the sailor swam to shore.

He stood, glistening in the sun, and held out the square of wood. The chief took it from him. He glanced at it. He passed it back to the villagers. They shook their heads. They could make nothing of it. (The deep knife-scorings on the wood were different from the delicate scratches of the cripple one.)

The harper studied the message; he could make nothing of it.

The sailor stood in the shallow water, wringing water out of his russet beard.

'With one stroke from my hammer,' said the blacksmith, 'I could send this dragon-man to join his fathers and grand-fathers.'

The sailor stood there as if he half expected to be transfixed by a dozen spears: but quite indifferent. Death, or a gift of fish: it was all one to him.

Meantime the cripple scribe was furrowing his brows over the marks on the wood. He too was having difficulties with this language. Occasionally he paused and nodded, then frowned again. A dog barked from the side of the mountain. The sun took a short step down the sky.

Then, suddenly, the face of the cripple one brightened. He laughed. He pointed to the writing on the wood and nodded at the stranger who stood there shivering with his feet among the reeds at the loch-edge. The stranger permitting himself a smile: it seemed likely now that the Picts would not make him into a criss-cross of spears after all.

The scribe read the message to the elder and the villagers: WE HAVE NOT SAILED FROM THE ICE BUT FROM SUNLANDS IN THE SOUTH AND NOW WE ARE SAILING HOME TO ORKNEY BUT WE HAVE LITTLE FOOD AND NO FRESH WATER AND WE WILL GIVE YOU IN EXCHANGE THE DANCING SUN WATER CALLED

WINE LET THERE BE PEACE BETWEEN THE SHIP AND
THE VILLAGE

The girl walked down to the sand and threw a wolf-skin
over the shivering sailor. The elder kissed him on the cheek.
The sound of cheering reached the mountain caves; they
could see the women hurrying down, eager to hear the news,
so eager not to miss anything that they left the children and
the old ones trailing far behind. The mountain side was
tremulous with bewildered sheep.

Now at the prow of the ship the sailors had set two wine
barrels.

'Consider,' said the artist-scribe to the harper, 'in future we
will be able to trade with ships that come from far away –
from Ireland, from Brittany, from Cornwall. All that's
necessary is that the helmsman on the ship, or the merchant,
has enough imagination to understand our signs.'

'Imagination is not given to everyone,' said the harper.
'Lately I have fallen in love with the falconer's second
daughter. She is much younger than me – hardly more than
a girl. She would laugh at me – so would all the villagers – if
this was known. I suffer very much.'

'Not only trade,' said the cripple. 'Think of the riches
that will belong to the tribe, now that we have discovered
that sign and speech are one. The legends, the great heroic
stories, the chants – we had to depend on the old men to
remember them, and much was lost, every generation a
little more was lost, or changed, or debased. Some of them
are no more than nonsense, now. The pure original epic of
our people is very much worn. But now there will be no
more wear-and-tear of that most delicate fabric, for we will
be able to write the stories down. Not yet. There are things
that my picture-speech can't do. But I have made a start.

Other scribes, makers of signs not yet born, will go further than me.'

'That girl!' said the harper. 'I didn't think I could ever suffer so such pain here, in my heart, because of a girl! Two years ago she was a child, picking flowers and shells. I saw her and I didn't see her. Now she has taken possession of me utterly. She may be a witch.'

'The laws too,' said the scribe. 'They work, in a way, but they are rough-hewn and crude. So much compensation for a stolen sheep, so much for a net wilfully damaged, so much for a net accidentally damaged, so much for assault, so much for a man-slaying. But the whole system is so complex that the old chief at the law-meeting throws up his hands in despair. He is unable to unravel the ancient judgments. No longer. The laws will be written down on a parchment, straightforward and plain. Every man will know how he stands with regard to the law.'

'The strange thing is,' said the harper, 'I have made more beautiful songs this past month, since that slut of a girl bewitched me, than ever I made before. Love is a great mystery. I enrich the four winds with the pain of my harpstrokes.'

'There remains a great deal to do,' said the scribe, 'before the art of writing is perfected. Simplified pictures – these are not enough. I spoke long to the man from the Orkney ship. That is to say, we didn't exactly converse, because our languages are different. But we gestured, we used eye-speech, we drew very intricate and beautiful pictures with a stick on the sand. This scribe from the north told me an interesting thing. In Norway men have devised another kind of script. The letters in this script are not visual representations; each letter corresponds to any and all the sounds a man might make with his tongue, teeth, lips, throat, palate – the beautiful liquid sounds, bird song, burn water – and also the sounds that are hard as stones, and sharp as axes.'

'I am growing old,' said the harper. 'Why should a grey-beard like me suffer because of a girl? I chanted those love-lyrics to the assembled villagers a few nights ago. Those who know about such things said the poems were beautiful – the most beautiful I had ever made. One or two of the people were in tears. I looked at the girl as I sang, as I struck my harp. Half way through the second lyric she got to her feet and ran out into the wind and the stars. She who had wrung those heart-cries from me. An ignorant stone-hearted girl! Yet I would give her everything I own. I would be glad to die for her.'

'When you think of it,' said the scribe, 'there are not many sounds that a human mouth can utter, little more than a score. So, said the scribe from the north, each sound will have its own symbol. "Think," said he, "of a tree with branches" . . . Each sound is to be like the trunk of a tree with branches radiating from it, right or left, one or several. The written tree-language he called "runes". When you look at the matter from their point of view, this deriving of an alphabet from a tree is most beautiful and fitting, because (according to the tribes of the north) the whole universe is nourished and supported by the great ash-tree Yggdrasill; its roots and foliage are deathless . . .'

'My heart is broken with beauty and pain,' cried the harper.

'Those lyrics of yours,' said the scribe, 'as soon as they are uttered they are blown away like petals, they are lost. Once the art of writing is mastered, poems will be more than flowers that unfold and then blow away on the wind. Every syllable will be cut deep in stone. The poems will last for ever, almost. But we do not have that skill yet.'

The harper went away, shaking his head.

The artist-scribe was alone.

He could hear the girl, calling his name from the mouth of the cave.

He lifted a stone from the ebb. A million movements of water had worn the red stone round and smooth. He carried the stone to the grass above and set it down. Then he hirpled to the smithy, and asked for a tool – a wedge of iron with a biting edge to it. It was getting late. A black cloud covered the sun in the west. He set about the lump of sandstone with controlled fury, striking the blunt end of the chisel with a chunk of rough granite, setting the edge here and there, positioning, striking and striking, till small pieces of sandstone sang about his head like bees.

The girl's voice sounded closer.

A shower of rain washed the red dust from the stone.

Delicately he loosened one or two last flakes. Then it was finished. Would people see anything in this whirl and tumult – a seeming chaos of incisions?

'Here you are,' said the girl. 'It's late. It's raining. Do you want to catch your death of cold? I've put on a piece of fish to boil for you.'

'This is for you,' said the scribe, pointing to the rough-tooled stone. 'For years you have given me fire and food. I keep sending you away. Always you are there, in the cave mouth, late and soon. Take this – it's all I can give you. It is you.'

'It's a stone rose,' said the girl.

The first star glimmered in the dews of the cut stone.

The Masked Fisherman

A crofter-fisherman belonging to Sumburgh in Shetland stood beside his boat that was hauled high on the beach. Sometimes he looked up at the shallow cliff and the cliff path leading from the road above down to the boulders and the sand. Sometimes he looked at the sea. The wind had whipped up the waves; white crests flew here and there. It might come to a storm – there was no telling. The sooner the lines were set the better. But the man who worked the boat with him hadn't come – he was late – very likely he had been drinking in the ale-house beyond midnight.

One thing was sure: Guthorm couldn't fish by himself, especially in such a rising wind. And if he couldn't put to sea, it would be a hungry weekend for himself and those squalling children. Gilli the tosspot: he kept a wife and three sisters and an aged toothless granny and two daughters, one dark and one fair. They never starved: drunk or sober, Gilli always managed to scrounge or steal or borrow enough to keep the sea fruit in their mouths, even if it was only a cod's head stuffed with liver and oatmeal.

Why did Guthorm share the boat with Gilli? He liked the man, for all his unreliability, for all his laziness, for all his lies. How comes there ever to be affection between one man and another – even between a good man and a sly shiftless man? Guthorm thought, *He makes me laugh, that Gilli* – all those stories about the women in his household and their ways and

words with each other and with the world: yes, but whenever
Gilli sat down at fire or at board, how all his women from the
oldest to the youngest turned their faces against him, and
soon railed at him in one wild discordant chorus! The good
fisherman could not but laugh at Gilli's stories – and whether
they were true or false made no difference, the laughter
leavened the dullness and dutifulness of his days.

Well then: the wind was rising, the now favourable tide
would soon be on the turn. Gilli had let him down again.
Gilli was lying in a drunken sleep that not even the seven
fierce-tongued women could break.

There was the rent to pay to the laird, taxes to the earl.
Those hard men took no account of ill-luck or incapacity.
Their due of fish had to be laid at the heraldic door of the
Hall, in foison or in famine.

Guthorm left the boat and began to walk up the beach. And
there, coming down the path from the road above he saw a
young man. Old Guthorm squinnied at him: he knew every
man in the parish by his walk and the set of his shoulders: but
this man was a stranger. As if to emphasize his anonymity, he
was wearing a hood that half covered his face. He approached
Guthorm with a lithe sure step: he was used to going on
seaweed and on great boulders, that much was sure.

'What's wrong, old man?' he called as he approached. 'It's
a good fishing day! Why have you turned your back on the
sea?'

The music his mouth made, that was strange too: but it
was agreeable, very pleasant, it had a lilt to it – and it seemed
neither inquisitive nor over-familiar nor hectoring. It was as
one honest man speaks to another.

'I should be fishing,' said Guthorm, 'and I would be
fishing, but my friend who shares the boat with me, I think
he isn't very well today.'

'Let me take his place,' said the stranger. 'I know a thing or two about the sea and the ways of fish.'

There was something very likeable about the young man – Ah, he would have liked such a one for a son! But his daughters were still at the age of playing 'trolls and princesses' in the little kale-yard of Quoy. And hungry they would be, and their thin washed-out mother, and himself too, if the boat wasn't launched sometime today.

'You can come and welcome,' said Guthorm.

Together they pushed the little yole out into the waves.

How Guthorm wished, before the fisherman's sun had climbed but a few golden steps up the sky, that he had kept his little boat noust-bound that day. It was a coarse-looking craft, lying under the rock – but once afloat it was a delicate dancer. For his guest, sitting at the oars, kept edging the boat in among the fiercest darkest tide-swirlings of Sumburgh. Ah, his boat – as desperately he leaned over the side and hauled in haddock after haddock – how often in the next hour he thought it would be upset, and himself and the white-cowled stranger thrown out and drowned, and their bones gathered forever into fiercest salt shuttles! Time after time, as Guthorm dragged in more fish still, he cried over his shoulder to the oarsman to have a care! to get out of these dangerous whirls and swirls into calmer water! . . .

Either the younger man was deaf or mad; for, if anything, he set the bow further in towards the deepest vortices of the tide-race, and Guthorm was thrown back and fore among the thwarts – never however letting go of his line that still as he hauled it in, burgeoned with ever more splendid fish. But what is the good of a magnificent catch, thought Guthorm, if you drown before you can eat it? And, wedging himself agaisnt the stern-thwart, he unhooked the strongest flash-ingest cod he had seen all that summer.

Now the boat was whirling and plunging in the tide-race, well into it, and the oarsman was standing up and laughing as he tugged at this oar or that, guiding Guthorm's yole into the black turbulent heart of the stream where, it seemed, the strongest sea creatures pastured. (So Guthorm thought, but all his sea-life he had kept prudently to the edges: where, up to now, he had pulled in a sufficiency.)

Cod after splendid cod, and once an immense halibut! The bottom of the boat had layers of shrugging twisting fish now, slowly stilling and tarnishing. Guthorm thought, as he dragged another cod from the hook: 'This is the day of my death, for sure! How strange, the sea is giving me more treasure today than ever before. It is sad, my children and that poor wife of mine won't know anything about it. This huge haul of fish will sink to the bottom with me. How those little orphans of mine will have to pick about in the ebb for whelks and mussels! They'll never know what a rich splendid fish-erman their father got to be on the day of his death! It is sad indeed' . . . Even while Guthorm was thinking those things, he was aware of a surge of joy rising through him. Surge after surge, a reckless gaiety in his veins responded to the tumult of the waters. Spindrift clung to his beard, his arms to the elbows were blue and chilled, fish by fish he thumbed and flung from the hooks (only a hook here and there was empty); and Guthorm heard strange sounds issuing from his throat. He was laughing out of deep enjoyment for the first time since the grey and silver had come into his black beard. In the sagas, it was chanted that this hero and that had gone to his death, in battle or in tempest, laughing!

'They'll never believe,' he thought, 'that Guthorm, the gloomy old crofter of Quoy, died like a hero!'

A splendid cod yelled soundlessly from its torn mouth, and was thrown (threshing) on the heap.

Who were those people standing on the shore? Guthorm flung spray from his eyes, and saw Gilli's women, the old and the young, standing at the big rock. Gilli's mother had her hands raised sky-ward, like a sybil. Oar and rowlock whirled up and hid them: another wave, and those women teetered in a full pellucid prism between sun and sea and stone: till another thong of spindrift cut Guthorm across the eyes.

'I think there are not quite so many fish now,' he said.

So suddenly that it startled him, the mad thing of a boat rode placid on a slow pulse of sea. Guthorm pulled in naked hooks.

'That was good fishing, old one!' said the stranger. 'Well done.'

He dipped the oars, making towards the noust and the rock and the waiting women.

'You swine!' Guthorm yelled at him. 'You scoundrel! Thief and murderer! You all but made a widow and orphans today! Fool that you are, you know nothing about the dangerous waters out there. Have you never heard of Sumburgh roost? If I was a younger man, I would settle things with you – I would – be sure of it – before this day's sun went down! What kind of a man are you, anyway, muffling up your face in that hood? Not a monk, that's for sure. An outlaw, likely, that daren't show his face like an honest man!'

The boat rattled over the tidal stones, thudded gently and whispered on the sand. The fisherman and the stranger leapt ashore. Together they shoved and hauled the yole up the noust to the sheltering rock. It was twice as heavy now with its weight of fish.

The sky between sun and sea was a madhouse of gulls: a thousand flashing intersecting screaming arcs, circles, dips, flurries.

Gilli's women came about, but not too close on account of the stranger. One had a deep straw basket. Three carried sharpened knives.

'What are you wanting here?' cried Guthorm. 'There's no fish for you, not out of this boat! Go home, tell that drunkard of yours that I – that's to say, my friend here and I – have caught the biggest haul of fish that Shetland has seen this summer. See if that news will cure Gilli's hangover. Ale and fishing don't mix – tell your hero that. My friend here and I will divide the fish between us. So, off home with you, eat limpets and kale blades – that's all I have to say.'

But already the stranger was dividing his share of the catch among Gilli's women. With shameless hands they plucked the fish from him.

Turning to go, the shore breeze took the man's cowl and blew it back. His hair streamed out, gleaming. And an incense came from it – it enchanted the women's nostrils, fleetingly! The locks had been artfully cut, the curls (wind-lifted for a moment) stirred in bright cold clusters: not at all like their men-folk's cropped greasy shocks and stubbles.

Quickly the man pulled on his cowl again, as if anonymity was necessary both to himself and them.

The stranger walked up the sand-cut path towards the road. Lithely and easily he went: again, not at all like the crofters and fishermen who, after a morning's fishing, still kept for a time the sea-and-boat lurch and stagger. (Moreover, after the age of thirty or so, they began to stoop between plough and nets, thrawn and thwart with labour.)

And there, suddenly, the stranger was, sprawled on his face, his fingers clutching at tussocks of sea-pink and dock-ans! He had not looked where he was going – as folk who fish regularly for a living do – and he had stepped on a tassel of wet sea-weed.

At that, Gilli's fool of a wife began to cackle with mirth. She threw back her head and the strings of her neck tautened and she laughed, skirl after skirl.

The hooded man picked himself up. He turned and waved back at the woman. His teeth shone in the sun.

'You're a lot of trulls,' said old Guthorm to the women. 'But for that man it would have been a poor hungry weekend up at Gilli's house. Get home with you. Tell Gilli, I'll be looking for another man to go fishing with after midsummer.'

That same evening when the fishing women of Sumburgh were splitting and salting the day's catch, Einar of Gulberwick, a laird, rode down to the shore. The women turned their backs on Einar: one of them spat. Einar was not well-liked by the common people. He was only happy when he was among men of rank and valour: councillors or merchants from Norway and Scotland. A surprising thing it was that Einar had come now and reined in his horse beside women stinking with fish guts. That he should speak to them was a thing unknown hitherto.

'Which of you women was it?' said the laird. 'One of you women did this terrible thing. It was enough to make my cheek blanch, hearing it. Are you not afraid of justice and punishment?'

Gilli's old granny turned and faced him. 'What are you talking about?' she cried. 'Have we stolen? Have we slandered the king or the bishop? Leave us alone.'

'Where did you get all those fish?' said Einar. 'Not from Gilli – he's been sleeping all day.'

'A man gave them to us,' said Gilli's tall black-headed daughter. 'A stranger that took Gilli's place in the yole this morning.'

'So,' said Einar, 'this man gave you all that fish. And one of you – some ignorant thankless hag – laughed at the man when he slipped among sea-weed. Do you not know who he was, that man?'

'His face was hidden,' said Gilli's cripple sister. 'He didn't speak like us.'

'That man,' said Einar of Gulberwick, 'is his grace the Earl Rognvald Kolson, lord of Orkney and Shetland and Caithness and Sutherland. That man is the living nephew of Magnus, our saint! To sneer at such a man, the way you did, is next door to treason. Earl Rognvald is my guest up at Gulberwick. Earl Rognvald could, if he liked, put you out on the roads to beg! I am very displeased.'

'Tell the earl we did not know,' said Gilli's wife. 'We're sorry. Tell the earl that.'

'*I* am displeased,' said Einar. 'But the strange thing is, Earl Rognvald has been relishing the insult all day! He is a strange man, Earl Rognvald. He has been making a poem about the incident all day, and laughing as he sets the hard stony sounds among the stream of the vowels.'

'I never thought,' said Gilli's wife, 'that I would ever be put in a poem!'

'So it was you that laughed,' said Einar. 'Let me think. The subtleties of a poem are lost on the likes of you. The earl – my guest – has studied the art of poetry long and hard. I don't understand poetry very well myself. Still, I am honoured that a poem should have been made under my roof by such an illustrious man. But I wish he had chosen a nobler theme.'

'You're lavish with words,' said Gilli's eldest sister, a tart one. 'We'd rather be hearing the poem.'

'It goes like this,' said the horseman.

The hooded fisherman,
   down on his face he goes.
Down among sand and seaweed
   he fouls his clothes!
From an old girl in the fish-gleams,
   mockery rose.
An earl in a fisherman's coat,
   who knows, who knows?
From mingling of lord and lieges
   a good grace grows.

The women listened, wondering.

'I like that,' said Gilli's wife, 'better than all his fish. Tell Rognvald Kolson that.'

Sylvanus, A Monk of Eynhallow

And in the evening they came to a small dark island among many islands.

And there a girl met them on the shore, but her words were strange. Sven said to Ragnar then, 'I have seen this girl before. The girl has seen us too. I am glad now that she does not recognize us.'

The girl pointed at a small house of turf and stone with rafters of wood newly charred.

There they slept that night. It rained. 'That is our bath for this year,' said Ragnar when they woke. 'The wound in my neck hurts me a little.'

The girl brought them shell fish. They left the empty shells on a stone. They rowed north.

There were not many people to be seen anywhere on the shore.

In the afternoon they came on a little monastery on a headland. The walls were black, the red tongues had licked them well.

'I think we should row on,' said Sven.

They heard a sound of axes among the trees. Presently one of the monks came in sight dragging a tree; he laid it among other dressed trunks against the roofless wall.

The monk was singing in Latin. He was a strong cheerful young man.

'Here we have been also,' said Sven to Ragnar.

There was a new-made grave mound and a new white cross had been set up.

'There are eight monks lying in that howe,' said Sven.

'I did not think one had escaped,' said Ragnar.

'Farewell, voyagers,' cried the young monk to the boatmen.

They were very hungry on the third day. They tried to catch fish with their hands, but one fish and then another flowed through their fingers.

'I think even the fish here have come to dislike us,' said Ragnar.

'What our people have done wrong', said Sven, 'for a hundred years is to try to force the creatures within the circle of our hungers. Strike them down coldly, as a man would break a stone to build a wall!

'The people of the west, they live in friendship with the animals. *Friends, we are hungry,* they might say.

'*Come now within the circle of our hunger.* It seems then they come gladly. I have seen it happening. *Come otter, come wolf, it is winter, we are cold.* The beasts seem glad to give their coats to men. No animal wishes to die, but there can be a courtesy about death and even a kind of sanctity. Stones and clouds are living things too. When their masons cut a stone, it seems as if they bless the stone with every hammer-stroke. But we of the north have made ourselves men of pure and utter violence, alone among the creatures.'

'You talk too much,' said Ragnar.

They put their hands here and there in the sea. The fish would not come to them. Or if one came, it flowed easily out through their fingers.

The next morning at sunrise they did go ashore on a lonely beach for limpets and seaweed. They ate till their bellies were tight and cold.

'We will be thirsty after this,' said Ragnar.

They climbed up towards a well on a ridge, but soon heard from the hidden part of the island noises of lamentation and sorrow. Ragnar turned and fled down to the boat, and Sven followed. They pushed off. In mid-sound they looked back. A man with a hawk on his wrist was standing beside the well. The fowler shook the bird from his wrist, and the hawk rose against the sun and circled and came and stood above the two men in the boat. The hawk stooped until it was level with their faces. They could see its yellow eye glaring at them.

Then the bird swung off in its circle back to the fist of the fowler.

Cries of anger came from the shore. Gaelic fisherfolk shook their fists at Sven and Ragnar.

'It has come to a poor pass,' said Sven, 'when we are terrified of a fowler and a fish-wife or two.'

Ragnar muttered something about a drink of sea water, only a handful.

Sven said he had seen a man drink the sea off Rockall. The man had died two days later, raving.

'It rained three nights ago,' said Ragnar, 'when we were sleeping in that hovel. Why doesn't it rain now?'

'It seems,' said Sven, 'that not only animals and fish but all of nature has turned against us. Sun and rain and thunder, do they have thoughts of vengeance? Their ways are not our ways. But there may be connections that we do not understand. So, we take torches and burn simple people out of their huts. And now the sun is scorching our throats. There is a kind of justice in that. And lately we have thrust peaceful sailors back into the sea and drowned them. And now the other water, the sweet waters of burn and well, are forbidden us, and our tongues are like dry rags. We trample their green corn. *No bread,* says the kindly earth, *there shall be no bread for men who do such a thing . . .'*

'You speak like a preacher,' said Ragnar. 'I am sick. Be quiet.'

'There's a puff of wind now at sunset,' said Sven. 'I will raise the piece of sail that's left.'

'I think I hear the Pentland Firth in the north-east,' said Ragnar. 'One of us should try to stay awake all night. The wound in my neck has opened again.'

The sun went down, and it was very cold on the sea.

They heard in the north-east distance the bell noises of the Pentland Firth – slow and dark and wandering – the slow booming near and far of the bells of the Pentland Firth between the two great oceans – the slow surge and swing and outcry of the bells tolling and reverberating among the islands, under the stars, in the falling darkness. 'Try to sleep,' said Sven to Ragnar. 'We are not far from home. I will sit all night at the steering-oar.'

It seemed to Sven that they came to a very small island with a well in the middle of it, and cornfields all around. Then it seemed to Sven that they made the boat fast at a rock, and Sven and Ragnar went up to the well. Three children who were there came and stood in front of the well and held out the palms of their hands against Sven and Ragnar. And it seemed to Sven that the voices of those children were like harp-strokes.

The first child said, 'For war-men, the well is full of blood.'

The second child said, 'For most people, the water in the well is tasteless, a small invisible trembling in the sun, a nuisance mostly, all wetness and cold, except when there's a long drought.'

The third child said, 'This well, to the innocent and the good, brims with living water.'

Then the well and the children vanished, and nothing remained with Sven but a deepening thirst and echoes of the three-fold harp music. It lingered in his mind long after the dream had faded. The black bells of the sea surged and tolled all around the boat.

By morning they were clear of the Pentland Firth and drifting along the south shore of Hoy in Orkney. Sven guided the boat to a beach.

'I am holding the boat for you,' said Sven to Ragnar. 'Try to step ashore.'

But in the end he had to drag Ragnar ashore on his shoulder, and set him down under a rock.

Sven did not bother to make the boat fast but left it stottering and stammering on the stones of the ebb.

Sven knelt down and soaked his face in a cold tassel of seaweed. He discovered a little rill among the rocks. He invited Ragnar to drink before he did – 'not out of goodness,' said he, 'but if a man denies himself a little while, nectar and mead taste all the sweeter' . . . Sven cried out with the pain and the joy of the little spring.

But Ragnar showed no inclination to drink.

Presently a man came down the beach and told Sven to go away. 'Take that ruckle of a boat and row as far and as fast as you can. The laird up at Melsetter, he doesn't care for tramps hanging about his fields and beaches.'

'Tell Magnus Grayling of Melsetter,' said Sven, 'we have news out of Scotland about his longship *Raven.*'

'Get out quickly,' said the laird's man. 'I will set the hounds on you.'

Other men and women came down to the shore and stared at Sven and Ragnar.

The laird's daughter Signy had a grey-blue pigeon called Pax. Pax flew down from the dove-cot above and sat on

Sven's shoulder and put its beak into Sven's beard as gently as if it was feeding him crumbs and bits of fish.

Soon the laird's grieve came on the scene. He looked down at Sven for a while. Then he stooped and dragged aside the filthy curtain of Sven's hair and looked into his eyes.

'Sven Arnison,' said the grieve, 'you smelt sweeter the day *Raven* was launched. What happened?'

When the grieve looked down at Ragnar he saw at once that Ragnar was dead.

Sven slept up at Magnus Grayling's hall for a day and a night.

Then he got up and washed himself well and combed his hair and beard.

Soon after that Signy came and kissed Sven and brought him to the long bench where Magnus Grayling was carving a haunch of venison.

'Three weeks ago I was moderately well off,' said the laird. 'Today I'm next door to ruin. I expected great things from the cruise of *Raven*. Now I see she had a crew of fools and cowards. Sven Arnison, you will be marrying the daughter of a poor man.'

'Father,' said Signy, 'you have a dozen horses and a hundred cows and hillsides covered with corn. And three good ships.'

'Speak when I give you leave,' said Magnus Grayling.

'I will be a laughing-stock as far as Iceland on account of *Raven* and her voyage,' said Magnus a while later.

'I would like to work in the fields from now on,' said Sven. 'And then come home from the plough to sit beside the fire my wife has lit.'

'I will keep it burning for you, never fear,' said Signy.

'To think,' said the laird, 'that experienced Orkney seamen would fall into a trap like that! I have lost two good shepherds and four fishermen and the young man from the mill. That is worse, in a way, than losing *Raven*.'

'Furthermore,' said Sven, 'if Signy and I are not fated to sit beside the fire together, I tell you what I would do. I would go and see the abbot at Eynhallow and ask him to make me a novice. I have been thinking much lately. It seems to me that the world is full of unimaginable terrors and beauties. We are afloat, birth to death, in a great ocean of mystery.'

'Signy,' said Magnus Grayling, 'pour ale into his cup.'

The Nativity Bell and The Falconer

Fergus and the seven brothers who were left stood in the door of the little monastery of St Peter. The seamen from the east had put great wounds upon it, three Easters since. Many windows were broken. The fires had lapped the walls of refectory and dormitory and had broken through those roofs; the tapestry was torn from the chapel wall; the statues of the Queen of Heaven and St Peter were overset and scored with axe-gashes; chalice and candlesticks stolen. But the chapel roof was intact. The bell hung in the belfry still, a heavy flower.

Father Fergus had rowed across from Eynhallow island at dawn. Their little ox-hide boat lay high on the beach, safe from the pealing waves.

A seal watched from far out on a skerry.

Their curragh had been seen out in the sound, crossing over. Singly, and in small groups, the islanders now came slowly towards the monastery.

'Who knows?' said Fergus. 'They may be glad to see us. It is midwinter, Yule. They may want us to go away at once. Our little Celtic communities always drew the longships. We excite the viking greed. Our silence irritates them.'

The islanders approached slowly. They were both glad and afraid. 'Oh,' said the oldest man, 'what would we do now in mid-winter, at the year's death, without your bell and your psalms, and your story of the birth in the cowshed?'

'You'll have them,' said Fergus. 'Tonight at midnight is the time. Darkness and winter and death will be put to flight. We will celebrate the Nativity here once more.'

The islanders were glad. Silent joy passed from face to face. Even the face of the youngest child, carried by his mother, smiled.

'It isn't possible, Father,' said the old man. 'I must tell you this, the Norsemen are in the island now. Surely you have heard it, in the other monastery in Eynhallow where you have been since you were driven out, that terrible plough-time? A longship came a week ago. There was no harrying and burning and going away again. They have taken over the big farm at the east shore of the island. That was my farm before the burning. They carried up ploughs from the ship. You can't see the ship from here, it is drawn up on the beach below the big farm. They have patched the roof of the farmhouse with clean Norwegian wood. We see smoke from the farm every night. We hear their shouts. We keep well to this side of the hill.'

'We will stay for this night,' said Fergus. 'We will celebrate the Feast of the Nativity. Perhaps we'll stay all the twelve days till the Feast of Epiphany.'

'I must tell you this,' said the old farmer. 'They have their axes too. Their longship has the dragon on it, breathing blood and flames. They have a man watching every day from the hilltop there. They know you and the brothers are here. Go now, before they sharpen the blades and light the torches.'

'Yes,' said a young man. 'It is great joy for us to have you here at midwinter. But there is too much danger.'

'They are a terrible people,' said the old man. 'One of them has lured the hawk out of the cloud and put a hood on it. The hawk hunts for them.'

'You are welcome to the Mass at midnight,' said Father Fergus. 'We have brought another chalice. The candles will burn in new tall silver.'

The old man turned, shaking his head. The islanders followed, singly or in groups, to their huts on the barren side of the hill.

The light was brief, between dawn and sunset. The Celtic monks set the chapel in order. They stretched sewn skins over the charred dormitory beams. It would be possible to sleep, if the weather continued mild and bright.

'What fools we are!' cried Brother Cormac. 'We have brought fuel but we have left the food and drink in Rousay.'

'Light the fire,' said Fergus. 'It will be a cold night. A fast won't hurt us.'

At noon the brothers saw a young bright-haired man, a stranger, down at the shore. He was speaking to the seal. The seal turned huge questing eyes on the man from the dragon-ship. It lifted its head.

At sunset the little community chanted the prayers and psalms in the hacked and burnt chapel.

They had set up the statues in their places, The Star of the Sea and The Fisherman.

The candles scooped shadows on their bent faces. The candles put a wavering brightness on their lifted psalming faces.

They trooped out of the chapel, slowly, one after the other.

They saw, against the sunset, on the hilltop, a single figure, watching.

'Oh,' said the youngest brother, beside the fire, 'I am hungry. We are all hungry.'

'There are people hungrier than us,' said Fergus. 'Every-where. Always. The innkeeper is turning the man and the woman away. *No,* he is saying, *I am full up. There's nothing for you* . . .

The boy wanted to say also that he was afraid. But Fergus, in that case, would say that fear was universal, but it could be overcome by love.

The boy started. There was a splash and a commotion at the shore below. 'It is the seal,' said the monk who stood at the door, keeping watch. 'All nature is full of the expectation of great joy.'

At Evensong, a few of the crofters and fishermen came in and knelt at the back of the chapel.

The candles burned like stars: pure cold flames.

The plainchant filled the chapel with such beauty that the old man whose farm had been taken, wept.

He said to Father Fergus in the chapel door, 'There's silence on the far side of the hill, in the farm. I am uneasy always when those men are silent.'

'Bring all the people at midnight,' said Fergus. 'It will be a joyful feast. You can bring your ox too and leave it at the door. The Feast is for all creation.'

It was a still evening. They could hear the seal plashing in the shallows.

'Don't ring the bell,' said the old man. 'That maddens them. They light the torches. They sharpen their axes then.'

The tongue of the bell kissed the rim, once, under the arch of stars, and circle after circle of sound went wavering over the island.

The boy pulled the rope, and the bell cried, and sent out richer circles of sound.

The bell nodded and cried in a regular rhythm, it pealed, it sent out joyful surge upon surge.

At the altar, Fergus lit the candles.

He turned and climbed the stone spiral to the bell-ringer. 'Well done,' he said. 'You made a good sound. You must come now and serve me at the altar.'

Outside in the darkness were stumblings and cries, a lowing and a whinny or two. Shadows loomed out of darkness. It was the Pictish folk, all thirty of them, from the elder with the harsh grey beard to a swaddled infant on its mothers back. And more than them. They were leading and driving the three oxen and the dozen goats. The fishermen carried their oars and lines. The youngest fisherman brought a gift of haddocks. The young mother presented goat cheeses. The doorkeeper accepted them at the door.

Some of the people were looking fearfully behind them, from time to time, into the darkness.

The great broken net of stars reached from horizon to horizon.

The night was very still, after the bell-summons. Then they heard the plash below, off the skerry.

'The seal isn't asleep either,' said the boy.

'Come into the chapel,' said Fergus to the folk. 'The unborn King will be pleased with your gifts. The animals will have to remain outside. The wonder will be for them too.'

The Celtic monks were already in their places in the choir, kneeling. Candle-light laved their bald bowed heads and clasped hands.

The thirty islanders knelt and crossed themselves (the crosses like shields in front of them, for defence).

Fergus and the young monk came and stood at the altar, with bread and wine and book, between the candles.

The Mass of the Nativity was about to begin.

The latch lifted. A star-cold air entered the chapel and the candle flames fluttered and then were still again.

A stranger with wings of bronze-gold hair about his shoulders, and a bronze beard, came in. He turned and beckoned. Other young men followed him: seven.

A stir of terror went through the islanders. They made raggedly, shields and crosses in the air, to defend them. 'The first one to come in,' whispered the old Pict, 'is the one who took the hawk from the cloud and put the hood on it.'

At the altar the priest read the opening psalms. The boy's hand, turning the page, trembled. The kneeling monks did not look round.

. . . *Filius meus es tu, ego hodie genui te. Quare fremuerunt gentes: et populi meditate sunt inania? Gloria* . . .

Two of the Norsemen were carrying awkward burdens. They set them against the scorched wall of the chapel.

Then all seven of the Norsemen came and knelt, one after the other, on the cold stones, between the islanders and the monks in the choir.

Outside, under the silver star-web, the ox bellowed once. A goat snickered.

The young monk looked once towards the corner of the chapel where the men from the dragon-ship had set down their burdens. A scattering of barley had fallen from the sack and lay about the floor. The great jar was full of mead – there was no mistaking the honey smell, the essence of last summer's bee-labour in the east, in a Norwegian flower-starred valley . . .

– *Dominus vobiscum*

– *Et cum spiritu tuo*

The islanders saw that the falconer, kneeling on the cold stone, had brought his hands together, and they seemed to make in the air the shape of a dove, furled.

Shore Dances

We are in serious trouble, here in the island.

They are in serious trouble, though they never had more coins to rattle in their pouches and to kist under the beds.

We are in serious trouble. Mr Sweyn the laird has been, and gone again, purple faced with wrath, to Kirkwall, to report to the authorities there. No doubt he will try to do his best for the islanders, and turn away wrath from their doors. But he cannot prevent the mockery that will fall about his own head.

The island woke at dawn, a week ago exactly, to see a three-masted armed ship anchored out in the bay, and a small boat rowing between ship and shore, with three men in her.

There was anxiety until it could be known what the ship was, and what she wanted. It was unlikely to be either the Press Gang seeking recruits, or sheep thieves or smugglers; they went about their business in the dark of the moon.

The boat grounded.

A young man stepped ashore.

The island men watched from behind rocks. Only Ran Eunson showed himself at the mouth of Rinians Cave: a huge powerful young man with fists like clubs and a voice like a trumpet. Ran hailed them.

What unutterably strange music was it that came from the sailor's mouth: a sweet strange incomprehensible jargon?

Hands accompanied the voice, fluid lucent shapes in the air. Poor Ran gaped at him.

Fish – it was obvious that the graceful young man from the ship wanted fresh fish. He sculpted fish with both hands. His right hand made undulations in the wind.

Ale – he drew a beautiful bottle shape in air, he tilted a cup, he made a small precise comical stagger on the wet stones.

Butter, cheese – he knew what went on in farms at milking time. He knew how churns are steered.

Water – when you think about it, it must be difficult to mime water. The sailor tilted his face skyward, he held out both hands. One could almost see the shine of rain, after a long drought, over cheekbone and knuckle; and his mouth imitated the gentle plangencies of water on grass and stone. And then, smiling, he pointed to the well above the shore. There was no doubt that the ship wanted water, and urgently.

Bread – he imitated a ploughman stumbling after an ox (the sea gleam on his face notwithstanding). He imitated a scytheman. He broke a round of air in two and put a fragment of delicious nothingness into his mouth.

Honey – he wore a bee-mask, he flung red-hot seething sun embers from his face. He sucked from his fingers delicious drops.

Now that the peaceful intentions of the ship in the bay had been made obvious, the island men rose up from behind their rocks, one after the other, and showed themselves without fear. Also Bella Swann came down from the field where she had been milking her father's cow. And an old man, Sander Groat, came hirpling rapidly on a stick along the shore road, in case there might be some free tobacco going. And Merran came from the fishing bothy, shawled, working lips and gums: to see, maybe, one marvel yet before the last marvel.

Apart from everything else, it had been a rare entertainment to see the slow dance and mime; and to hear the beautiful incomprehensible music from the harp of the stranger's exquisitely moulded mouth.

(All this was told me, starkly, in my study at the Manse, by Saul the shepherd before noon. Saul had seen the complete performance from beginning to end. Without Saul Birsa, Mr Sweyn and I would not know the half of what goes on here in the island.)

The young foreigner stood at last before them, all smiles and open palms. He had no more signs to make. Let there now be some kind of a reply.

The island men drifted together. It was obvious what the ship wanted. The next urgent question to be answered was, what would the island receive in exchange for bread, water, ale, fish, honey, cheese and butter?

James Tomison was appointed to negotiate on their behalf.

James Tomison stepped forward.

James Tomison made the action of opening a pouch and counting out a fistful of money: all urgent fingers and spread palm.

It was not such a fine mime as the young sailor's, by any means, but it was as effective in its way. James Tomison was only half through his reply when the stranger nodded eagerly, and laughed, and gestured to the sailor sitting in the stern.

That sailor brought from a belt hidden under his shirt a leather poke. He shook it; it rang like a bell. He loosened the thong. He poured a silver stream over the wet stones. The shore was possessed by a myriad flashings, by the ringing of many small bells.

I regret to say that, at this point, an island man who shall be nameless proposed to rush on the three foreigners at once and overpower them, then gather up the silver scatterings and share it out in equal parts.

However, the majority of the island men are honourable.

Within an hour a considerable store of the island's natural bounty was stacked high on the shore. Many buckets came heavy and brimming from the well. (By this time a second larger longboat had left the ship, with a lashing of empty water-barrels in her).

Until mid-morning, while the tide ebbed, the exchange went on: the loading of the boats, the picking of silver pieces large and small from rockpool and seaweed.

Never had the island men beheld such treasure. (In the sharing out, no doubt, there would be some trouble, a bloody nose and a thunder-laden eye here and there, and some small bitternesses that might outlinger the winter.)

Finally the loading was completed, the last ale-flagon stowed and the last water barrel lashed down.

The young man, his face grave now, bowed in acknowledgement of a fair day's trading. The island men answered with teeth-flashings out of their beards.

Oars were fitted in rowlocks. The blades made fine little singing circles. Two men strained at the bow to push off.

The young foreigner lingered still. He drew from his waistcoat pocket a coin that far outshone those that had hitherto enriched the morning. Even Ran Eunson the stupid giant knew gold when he saw it. The solitary piece flashed back from the sun into two dozen eyes. Then the Frenchman lifted his forefinger and pointed straight at Bella Swann, who was standing there on the road above with her milk-bucket in her hand.

Again, I am sorry to say that two or three men (I will not mention names) would gladly have taken that golden coin and afterwards thrust Bella in among the honeycombs and lobsters in the longboat. But Jimmy Ardale was there, fortunately, and at once he pranced about and threatened to put a knife into any man who wanted to go on with that particular piece of marketing. He flashed his knife round at the foreigner. Poor Bella didn't know what it was all about. When she heard the shouts down by the cave-mouth, and saw the glint of Jimmy's knife, she gathered up her summer-smelling bucket and made for the milking shed of Smelt: only once turning her comely face back. (All this Saul Birsa told me.)

At that smouldering and flash and outcry along the shore, the Frenchman didn't linger for another second. He made a sign. He vaulted lightly on board. With thew and oar-blade the longboats were thrust away from the stones and sand. A voice cried from the deck of the big ship. Voices answered from the two out-drifting boats. Laughter, made sweet and perilous on the harpstrings of the sea, passed between sailor and sailor.

'James Tomison, man,' I said in the kirk vestry later that afternoon, 'what were you thinking of, at all? You are a man of prudence and intelligence. Can it be you are not aware that the kingdom of Great Britain and the kingdom of France have been at war with one another since last March? I know not, James, what the end of this business will be. You have given aid and comfort to an enemy ship – no peaceful merchant either, for Saul tells me there was a line of black-mouthed guns along the hull of her. She was a fighting ship, James. That makes a difference, a very grave difference. James, technically you and all your fellow bargainers, that thought yourselves so smart this morning, may be traitors. I do not know – I am no lawyer. James, it may be you will need the bits of French silver to defend yourselves in the courts of admiralty. It is a bad business. Mr Sweyn must be told, of course. Why, man, did you not send up to the Manse if you were in any doubts about the legality of your proceedings this morning? No, you were too blinded with the shining and the music of all that silver. Good day to you, James Tomison. I have nothing more to say just now. I will write a letter with a full account of this incident to Mr Sweyn in Kirkwall. I hope Mr Sweyn will be willing and able to speak up for you. I fear, however, there are in Kirkwall men more powerful than Mr Sweyn your protector.'

Then, seeing how blanched the face of the poor man was, and how his hands holding his bonnet trembled like waterdrops, I said, 'Now, James, it may be all right. I think it will be all right. You do not read newssheets, you live in simplicity and ignorance, at the very extreme of the land. How should you know what nations are embattled, or what princes look coldly the one on the other? James, man, I will speak for you all to Mr Sweyn, and Mr Sweyn (I know it, though he will be troubled) will speak on your behalf to them that sit in seats of authority.

'After this, James, let all your dealings be with cornstalks and peat and cod-fish.'

The Scholar

There was this clever young lad. He won all the prizes in his island school. Then he went to the school at Hamnavoe and he won the prizes there. On he went to the college.

The island people said, 'What will he be? Will he be a doctor, or a lawyer, or a minister, or a teacher?'

He won the highest honour at the college in Aberdeen – 'summa cum laude' it said on the scroll.

The scholar returned to the island with a chest full of books. They said to him at the pier, 'What now, man?'

He shook his head and he walked home. His mother had a dinner of fish and potatoes on the table for him.

He was never seen outside again.

The island folk asked the mother how he did? She said to them, 'He sits at the table all night, writing words on sheets of paper. He sleeps all day.'

The mother worked for them both. The spinning wheel, the cow, the pig, the ox, the well, the peat-hill, even the plough and the boat – she went from one to the other to keep bread in the scholar's mouth and clothes on his back.

And she was growing old.

The scholar wrote and wrote in the yellow circle of lamplight.

His hair was growing long. There was a gauntness in his face.

One day on the peat-hill the old woman gave a groan. When the other peat-cutters got to her, she was on her knees. She gave another cry, and she died.

When the peat-cutters carried the body of the old woman home, her son was in his bed reading.

The sun threw a square of golden light on the stone floor.

A man said, 'Your mother, she's dead. She died up on the hill. We've brought her home.'

The scholar turned a page.

He said, 'Lay her over there. Tell the joiner. Tell the minister. Tell the grave-digger.'

He made a note in the margin of the book he was reading.

He did not even go to his mother's funeral. He said he was too busy. He pointed to the scattering of written sheets and blank sheets over the table.

But he kissed the cold hands of his mother before they nailed down the lid on the coffin.

He did not work on the sea or the land.

He grew thin and dirty.

He would have died in the darkening days if the woman in the next croft hadn't laid food at his door from time to time – bannocks, a fish, a poke of oatmeal, a dish of eggs, a pot of jam, milk.

He had not a word of thanks for her.

He never crossed the door for a bucket of water even. He stretched a cracked jug into the water barrel beside the door, and took it in, dripping. That was all that was seen of him, a long thin arm and a jug either dry or streaming.

But more than once a young man coming home late from his sweetheart's door would see a light in the window. Inside, the scholar sat at his table, writing, writing. Not even a tap at the window would make him turn his head.

A new schoolmaster came to the island.

The first thing they told him about was the scholar and his books and manuscripts.

The schoolmaster from Paisley knocked at the scholar's door one afternoon when the children were all scattered on the island roads going home.

There was no answer. The schoolmaster lifted the latch and looked in.

The scholar was in bed reading.

The schoolmaster greeted him respectfully. Then he introduced himself – 'I'm the new teacher.'

The scholar glanced up from his book to say, 'Go. Who asked you to come here? All you do is fill the heads of the children with nonsense. Get off. Close the door after you.'

Then he turned a page of his book.

The schoolmaster felt very hurt. He had been looking forward to having long conversations with the scholar on an evening now and then during the winter.

But he realized that he had trespassed on the man's privacy.

He lifted the latch to go.

The voice from the foetid bed said, 'Wait a minute. The schoolmaster, are you? You'll have a ream or two of paper in your classroom cupboard, eh? You'll have a big stone bottle of black ink. And more pens than you know what to do with. Good. I need some, urgently. I'm running short. Thank you. Close the door.'

Next morning a schoolboy left paper and pens and a medicine bottle full of ink on the scholar's doorstep.

*   *   *

Time passed. One day in the first snow a tinker girl knocked on his door, with a few cans and laces and ribbons for sale.

'Keep out,' the scholar called.

But the tinker girl went in, all the same, with sweet words.

She had never seen a householder like this – an ancient with a young face writing on a sheet of paper in bed.

A young voice said out of the filthy straggle of hair about the face, 'Go away. I need none of your trash.'

The tinker girl said, 'What are you doing, man?'

'I'm writing the wisest book in the world,' said the scholar. 'That was a whirl of snow over the floor then. Close the door behind you.'

The tinker girl left a red ribbon on the table – a gift for a poor crazy creature.

The kind neighbour woman, Madge, came two or three times a week.

In the end she had to put the spoon of porridge into his mouth, and the ale cup: while his eyes remained on the page he was reading.

'If I got some peace,' he complained, 'I would get this work finished before I die.'

Once, when he was asleep, Madge combed his hair and his beard. She trimmed the untidy fringes with scissors. She cut his fingernails.

'If only I could wash his hair,' said Madge, 'how beautiful and bright it would be, like sun on a cornfield!'

And Madge swept the stone floor and washed the curtains and kept a blink going in the fire.

'You're a nuisance,' said the scholar to her one day. 'I don't want to see you again, woman. You see that sheet of paper on the floor, with writing on it? Put it on the pile of papers on the table. Then go.'

'I'll be back on Thursday,' said the kind neighbour. 'What you really need is a good scrubbing from head to toe.'

The minister, black against the window, said, 'Your father and your mother, they had high hopes of you. Your father went to his grave happy in the knowledge that his clever son – you – would have a better and fuller life than he ever had.

'Your mother, that good soul, was rudely shocked before she died. I think you broke her heart, man.'

The scholar said, 'Listen, I didn't ask you to come here. I don't want you. You're wasting my time. Worse, your presence, like rust and moths, is devouring the great treasure I am hoarding in this place. Go.'

The minister said, 'Every man has one talent at least. You were given a brimming handful of rare talents. What have you done? You have buried them, hidden them away from the light. Only yourself can gloat on them, in secret. But the talent a man is given must be used for the good of all men, so that the whole world may be enriched thereby.'

'I don't know when the work will be finished,' said the scholar. 'I think I'll still be writing when I'm a hundred. It's going to be more difficult than I thought. I would read you a page or two, but you wouldn't understand.'

The minister rose to go, seriously displeased.

'The tinker lass who was here at the start of winter,' said the scholar, 'she would have understood a little, I think. I wish I had read a chapter to her.'

The minister left with such vehemence that the solid wooden door shook in its frame, and a few pages of manuscript fluttered down to the floor like white wondering birds.

In the month of January the scholar became sick. He coughed. His cheeks were two gaunt apples of fever.

All he wanted was water, water, water.

The heavy books fell out of his hands. His writing went like a slow crazy spider across the page before the pen too fell out of his furrowed fingers.

The kind neighbour Madge wet his lips with water. She wiped his brow.

'You see that book in the chair over there?' said the scholar. 'Read it – beginning of Chapter 5, page one hundred. I can still listen, even if I'm too weak to read and write.'

'I can't read,' said Madge. 'I did go to the school but I've long forgotten paragraphs and pages. I had better things to do.'

'Get out,' he said wearily. 'You're useless.'

That was the last words he spoke for a week, other than incoherent babblings, especially at night, when the illness blew up the flames in his body and then he would cry out in agony sometimes and sometimes in a kind of white trance.

In the morning his body was all grey ashes, a hearth on the verge of extinction: until Madge turned up with a cup of pure well water and fragments of white chicken in a bowl, which she put into his shrunken mouth.

With such attention she coaxed the scholar slowly back to life.

'Three weeks wasted,' was all he said. 'Thousands of golden words lost. Why do such things have to happen to me, when every minute is precious?'

'Birds and bairns and plants get sick too, sometimes,' said the kind neighbour.

And she gathered the scattered sheets of manuscript together and tied them with the red ribbon that was a gift from the tinker lass; and she put the pile in the cupboard.

* * *

Summer lengthened. He wrote and read incessantly, an urgent pilgrim on the road of Wisdom. Sometimes he laughed.

On the day of the Lammas Market all the young island men and women went down to the boat that would take them to Hamnavoe.

They went in their best holiday clothes. Pockets and purses jingled with money.

All the revellers were on board when a stranger stepped off the pier on to the *Orion*.

Who was he, at all? Where had he come from?

He was young and handsome, with a neat golden beard and a face shining from a basin of cold water. He wore, like all the young men, a dark mothball-smelling suit. His shirt and his black shoes were new.

The man paid no attention to the other passengers. He stood in the bow watching the cold cleavings of sea.

The old ship's-mate came round, half-way to Hamnavoe, to collect the fares: one shilling each.

He stopped in front of his passenger that nobody seemed to know. The old man stared into his face for a long time.

Then he said, 'Erlend Howe. I thought I saw your father's eyes and your mother's mouth. You're the one that read too many books at the college and went off his head. Well, boy, you look sensible enough now. I'm glad you've decided to take a day off.'

'Tell nobody,' whispered the scholar, and proffered the shilling for his fare.

Some islanders say they saw him all through that day at the Hamnavoe Lammas Fair: in the ale-booth, drinking beside the barrel – lifting the dark flap of the fortune-teller's booth – throwing wooden balls at coconuts – bringing down a wooden mallet so hard that a bell rang high above – watching the black 'prince of the Congo' licking with relish a red-hot poker. They even saw him speaking to Hamnavoe lasses, and offering them 'fairings' of chocolate or boiled candies. He moved alone through the music and the coloured streamers all day till the sun went down.

Other islanders say no: once he got off the *Orion* they never saw him again.

In the evening, after the flares were lit round the Fair, the tinkers drove into the town with kettles and pots, laces and herbs. A beautiful dark tinker girl went through the crowd offering red ribbons for sale.

Whether he was at the Hamnavoe Fair or not, the one sure thing is that the scholar disappeared completely from the island.

Madge went to his house on the Thursday morning.

There was no one there. The bed was empty. The books lay here and there about the floor like heavy dead birds.

Madge went to the cupboard where the piles of manuscripts were stacked. The shelves were empty.

It was then that Madge saw the choked hearth. Heaps of curled black trembling whispering ash everywhere: all that was left of the man and his labour.

'Well,' said Madge, 'he would have been warm and bright for an hour or so. He wasn't entirely witless in the end. Besides the burning, he put on a decent stitch to go on his journey, wherever that is.'

Not all the manuscripts had been given to the flames.

In a table drawer the young schoolmaster, summoned to gather the scholar's books so that they could be sold at the auction in Kirkwall, came on a sheaf of papers covered with signs (they could not be called writing). Squares, circles, semi-lunes, diamonds, wedge-shapes, arabesques, spirals, diagonals, black blocks, bright blocks, pentagons – page after intricate mysterious patterned page.

The schoolmaster folded the sheets with reverence and gave them to Mr Sweyn the laird. The laird stowed them in the great chest of writings where all the transactions of the island, with official seals and stamps and ribbons, had been hoarded for centuries against the uncomprehending slow siege of time.

'Where have I been?' said the tinker lass in the mill door. 'I'll tell you if you buy this mirror, mister. (It'll make your wife look twenty years younger.) This tin can here, you'll swear the laird never supped sweeter ale, nor claret nor whisky, out of his old silver quaich. One penny. Well, I've been to Wick and Ullapool and Strathnaver. (The mirror is threepence, twopence to you.) And then . . . Oh no, I won't say – it's a hard thing not to be believed. A drop of malt? Well now, mister miller, you're a kind decent man. Skol – I am looking at you through the glass of truth. Ah! The wandering? I took boat one cold filthy sleety day in January, and the boat never stopped rocking and plunging till it grounded on a rock in the west. Such a place! – the sour old boatman that ferried me – you'll never believe this – he stepped ashore as good-looking a boy as ever I winked after on the roads. Apple orchards and blue skies and shepherds and pipe-music. The people were all lovely and young and kind. It's no wonder the folk of Barra and Eriskay call that The Island of the Young. Mister, I never heard fiddle nor harp to equal the music of their speech. I thought I should stay there – hadn't I found a grey hair in my head the morning I sailed? and a small wrinkle or line of perishment in the skin of my forehead? . . . I thought Tir Nan Og would be a good place to wander in for

the rest of time. (No clocks nor calendars there, mister.)
Then, mister miller dear, who did I see but the book-crazy
chap that disappeared two Fairs ago? There he stood at the
shore, all yellow curls and laughter, among the young
welcoming ones. He had a long pipe in his fingers. His kiss
on my mouth was one of a score of kind kisses. And that
island greeting put me in mind of another poor grudging
loveless island with a minister and a miller, a dozen crofters
and seven fishermen, and their women, and a laird and a
schoolmaster and a broken-down sailor and a blacksmith
and a tailor and Jock the tramp, and a troop of bright bairns
that didn't know – poor things – what was coming to them.
And thinks I to myself, what way can I ever be long or far
from that crazy patchwork? There they are, on the road to
age and death and the kirkyard, and not a tin cup or a red
ribbon or a mirror or a fine story to cheer them. What would
I be without my pack and their grudging doors? Oh, I
couldn't endure it.

'A ribbon for your girl's hair, a ha'penny.'

The great stones of the mill thundered then, turning,
grinding out the bread of the island.

One empty house stood above the shore.

The tinker lass went out into the wind and the rain, less
burdened than she had come.

A Haul of Winter Fish

Storm and blizzard over Hamnavoe – storm and snow day after day as the light dwindled down towards midwinter.

The storm from the north had roused the sea to great snarling crested billows. It would have been madness for the Hamnavoe fishermen to put out in such weather. Hunger could be endured. The loss of men and fishing boats was a thing not to be thought of.

So the poor families ate the dried sillocks from last summer. The three shopkeepers would give them no more credit; there was enough debt against the fishing houses in their ledgers.

No good going to the farms and crofts round about. The crofting families were as poor as themselves, almost.

The storm raged on. At night, during a blizzard, one Hamnavoe house couldn't see the light in the window of the house on the next pier, through the dark whirls.

Time was like a wick in an almost exhausted lamp, as Yule drew close.

The time darkened down towards Yule.

The boy from the very poorest house in Hamnavoe was standing, after sunset, at the edge of his father's pier. In the lull between two blizzards a patch of sky had shredded thin. A star shone through rags of cloud, bright as a nail.

Beyond Hoy, he could hear the shifting muted thunders of the Atlantic.

The star put a thin lustre on the darkening heave of harbour water. The fishing boats were drawn high on the nousts, safe as gulls in crag crannies.

An abandoned hook on the edge of the small pier took the light of the star; the barb glittered diamond-bright for a second.

Then the wind roused itself with a clap of hands and a black yell.

The first flakes of a new blizzard danced all about the boy.

The star was quenched, suddenly.

He turned. He went into his house.

The family sitting round the hearth-fire turned flushed story-rapt faces to his cold face.

His mother said, 'So that's it – you'd rather be out in the black night than sitting with your family round the fire. At Yule too! A strange boy – you've always been a strange boy.'

He said nothing.

'There's no more food, the pot's empty! In the morning we're going to the Kirk Rocks for seafood. You'd better get to bed – it's an early start. Old grand-da's tired with telling stories.'

The boy brought the coldness and darkness of winter into the fire-circle and the story-glutted faces.

Grand-da, the harp of his mouth still trembling, lighted his pipe.

The fire fingered gold through the hair of the boy's three sisters.

The little one slept in his crib in a corner; time pulsed softly through him, like fish in the fathomless depths.

'There's one piece of news', said the boy. 'I saw a boat. It came out of Hoy Sound into the harbour just at the time of the first stars. I never saw that yawl before. A black man came up the steps of our pier, he was carrying a heavy basket of fish. He shouted to two men in the boat below. They passed up to him two more baskets of fish. The black man set the three baskets on our pier. He never said a word. Then he and the two other foreign-looking men (one with a gold ring in his ear) walked on up to the ale-house. And that's the end of the story.'

'Get to your bed,' cried the mother. 'You and your dreams! Some fisherman you'll be when you grow up. To bed with you. It's an early start for us all. A seaweed dinner for Yule, if we're lucky' . . .

When the mother opened the door in the morning, upon the jet and crimson of dawn over Scapa, there were three brimming baskets of cod on the pier: enough to feed every house in the village.

The storm was over – the harbour flashed, all azure and silver.

Her cry of amazement brought all the family to the door – three sleepy-eyed yellow-haired girls, the bitter fisherman who had caught no fish since December came in, old grand-da with his pipe in his hand.

Inside the child cried: a small star of wonderment.

From the neighbouring piers groups of fisher folk watched.

They called – bright shivering words. They held out their hands towards the baskets of fish.

Only the boy slept on in the box bed – the dreamer – as if he had been drawing in heavy lines all night in a rough sea westward.

Christmas Visitors

The last of my Yule visitors left at ten o'clock. Thorfinn put a big peat on the fire. 'Now that'll keep you warm till you go to bed! It'll still be burning in the morning when you get up – there'll be a red glow.'

Then Thorfinn my eldest son kissed me on the forehead, and went back to his wife, who has never entered my door for ten years past.

But Thorfinn and Margaret's two children had come in the morning, of course, first thing, with their toys and presents. Pathetic little creatures! – Their faces were flushed with excitement, their mouths brimmed over with chatter. They gave me a calendar they had made themselves, with the head of a collie on it cut out of a magazine. I gave them a pound each and a glass of ginger wine. Ah, if they knew what was in store for them: the wasted years, the husks and ashes, the salt.

And yet what more beautiful creatures, my grandchildren come in from the snow, laughing before the fire?

Harry and Sylvia put their warm red mouths against my cheek, and were eager to be out again in the snow.

And I was glad to see them go.

For I thought another visitor might come, as every year.

Loneliness is what I rejoice in now, that only: the one red-grey ember in the heart, that only a sea wind can stir into flame.

Ah, thistles, the sharp stones, salt pools, those grand-children would have to suffer!

(She nods in her rocking chair.)

A new flame curled a yellow tongue round the peat on the hearth.

Christmas brings a few to this house still, like birds round a broken bannock.

That woman from next door came about noon, with her English voice and her English palaver and gush. I forget her name even. She came to the island two years ago for a holiday, and 'Oh, simply fell in love with the place and the people at once!' . . . So, she bought the half-ruin of the croft of Combers and has spent thousands doing it up, 'in the old traditional manner, of course – what else?' – but that doesn't exclude a television and refrigerator, washing machine and central heating, and a telephone.

Separated from her husband in Birmingham – three grown-up children in different places on the globe – I have heard it all . . . She has knitted me a pair of gloves for Christmas, the tiresome woman.

And yet she has experienced miseries of which I know nothing.

There is a good-heartedness in her, buried somewhere under the gush and the flummery.

I greeted her, 'A Merry Christmas,' and I gave her a scallop shell taken from the sea bottom fifty years ago by a man called Samuel. She will crush out her cigarette ends in it.

They know well enough, in the farms and houses round about, that I want none of their geese and plum pudding and sherry: no invitations. A plate of my own oat bannocks and cheese, and a cup of milk – that's my Christmas dinner, and has been for years.

I was just brushing the last oat crumb from my mouth when Dawn, the ginger cat from the next farm, Colbister, came.

He shook a crumb of snow from a forefoot, delicately, in the door.

'If it isn't Dawn! What's Dawn wanting at a poor house like this, when there's goose-skin and cream in plenty up at Colbister? Well, Dawn, in the old days you'd have had a sillock or two. But there's been no fish in this house since Samuel's time. What, you could be doing with a piece of cheese? Well, then, take it.'

And the red cat ate a piece of my cheese from my fingers with the utmost delicacy and relish; and sat for five minutes at the fire blinking and washing his hind leg; and went, with the same silent courtesy as he had brought to my door.

(She drowses. The expected one is later this year.)

I think I slept in my chair most of the afternoon.

The fire sank. It was time to put a broken peat on. It was time soon to light the lamp.

I listened for a while to children singing carols in some European cathedral, on the wireless.

Such purity, such joy! The thistles, the salt, and the sharp stones, that is what you have to pay, later, for that early fountain of innocence.

Does a spring begin to flow again, late, very late, the winter before death perhaps, out of the drifted stones of the years! – a thin pure upwelling? I think not.

I had a fifth visitor. I heard a shuffle and a throat-clearing in the porch, and in he came, the oldest man in the island, Isaac, in muffler, bonnet, mittens and rubber boots.

'Isaac, what taks thee oot on a caald night like this? Thu'd been better aside thee fire. Sit doon, Isaac, till I pour thee a dram.'

When Isaac had half finished his dram he cleared his throat and he told me that once I'd been the bonniest lass in the whole island of Quoylay. 'Samuel, he was a lucky man to get thee,' says he. 'I wad have asked thee to merry me afore Samuel, only I was too shy. I just cam owre the hill to luk at thee for ten minutes or so.'

I never heard Isaac say so many words at one time. I had never got a better Christmas present in my life.

He emptied the last few whisky drops into his open mouth. Then he shambled to the door and said, 'Goodnight, lass'; and the snow and the stars took him.

(She drowses. The expected visitor has never been so late.)

Why are you so long in coming this year, Samuel? In the early years, the first grey light was hardly in the window, when you were there, pulsing from the vividness and pain of the sea! That such coldness should give me such joy! And there you stood, sea-taken one, with the piece of torn net in your hand: speechless. No words passed. We delighted in each other's company. Thorfinn and Billy and Andrew slept in their cradles, with their little gifts on the chair, to await the opening of their eyes, one after the other: sea orphans. Andrew had not been born when you went in at the door of salt.

You stayed, man, while I lit the fire and hung the kettle on the hook. You were still there when I returned from the byre with the pail of warm milk. It filled the room, the light of snow and milk and bread, slowly.

Then, perhaps, one of the children rubbed the honey out of his eyes – and then you were gone, for you would never wish to harrow a child with sea-loss on a Christmas morning.

I would say, 'It's three Yules since you were lost off Yesnaby, Samuel. It joys me to see thee again. But it would be better for thee to rest soon, man' – And found I was speaking to vacancy.

'Ten Yules since you were lost, Samuel . . .' 'Seventeen Yules . . .' 'Forty-two Yules.'

When you come today, young man out of the sea to visit this old woman with cow and cabbage patch, it will be forty-three Yules since you unmoored that boat for the last time.

I think my lover will not come tonight. I pray he will not come – and yet all my year, from seedtime to harvest, is a hunger for his coming. Of late winters, his comings have been tardier and briefer. Last Yule there was but a shifting gleam, like sun reflected from ice on the wall of the yard; he was gone before the words of welcome were out of my mouth.

'Rest in peace.' An old cavernous clay-smelling skull, I will visit nobody – unless earth and sea mell and marry at the end of time.

He has come to terms with the sea-girls, I think, at last. He will bide in their house.

At nine o'clock Thorfinn came (as I said) with a fancy-wrapped box of chocolates and a Shetland shawl – and said stale words and put the big night-lasting peat on the fire and set the cold star of his kiss on my forehead, and went away again.

(She is left with silence in the heart of her last winter: until the earth and the sea are one.)

Miss Tait and Tommy and the Carol Singers

There was a very severe old lady called Miss Tait who lived alone with her cat Tompkins in a big house at the end of the village.

All the village children avoided Miss Tait's house. She was especially severe if they came round on Bonfire Night, or to collect for charity – though it was well known that Miss Tait was the richest person in the island, by far. The tin tea caddies on her mantelpiece, it was said, were stuffed with musty-smelling moth-eaten twenty-pound notes. They put treacle on her door-knob at Halloween, and once they tied an empty tin to the tail of Tompkins the cat.

How enraged Miss Tait was! She phoned the island councillor, district councillor, J.P., and the police office in Kirkwall. But nobody could find out who the wicked young scoundrels were who had inflicted such mischief on Miss Tait and Tompkins.

Miss Tait found her grandfather's thick hickory stick in the attic, and blew the cobwebs off it. 'This,' said Miss Tait to Tompkins, 'is for the next young villain who comes round this house!'

And she made a fierce flourish with the stick until it whistled through the cold grey air of her kitchen.

Tompkins took one alarmed leap from floor to dressertop.

The air was cold because it was mid-December and Miss Tait had lit no fire since the miners' strike began.

*   *   *

The village children practised their carols, to sing here and there about the island two nights before Christmas.

All the children except Tommy practised their five or six chosen carols round the school piano, after four o'clock.

Tommy was not included because he had a voice like a crow; and, more than that, whenever the children did anything communally like a play or a bonfire, Tommy always ruined it with some piece of stupidity or clumsiness.

Two nights before Christmas, the choir, well muffled in bonnets and mittens and scarves, set out in lightly falling snow to sing their carols. How pure and sweet their voices sounded outside the inn, and at the teacher's house and the manse and the doctor's house – *Once in Royal David's City, Away in a Manger, O Come All Ye Faithful.*

As the choristers went through the falling snow to sing at their last station, the block of new council houses, one of them wondered where Tommy might be.

'Oh,' said Mary who had the sweetest voice in the choir, 'I saw him down at the shore, with a sack, just at sunset.'

After they had sung *Mary's Boy* outside the council houses – and got more 5p and 10p pieces, so that the collecting box rang like a bell – Willie (who was game for anything) said, 'Let's go and see what kind of a Christmas Miss Tait is having' . . .

That caused a fluttering among the girls! They had heard about Miss Tait's stick and how she meant to thwack boys and girls who came about her doors.

'It'll be miserable in there!' said Sandra. 'No Christmas tree. No decorations. Not even a fire!'

But, greatly daring, softly through the snow they stepped to Miss Tait's window and peeked through. They nearly fell on top of each other in astonishment! For who was sitting in

Miss Tait's armchair, eating an apple, but Tommy the out-cast! And there was a fire of wood in the grate, burning bright! And there was a sack of wood – shore-gathered – on the floor. And every now and then Tommy threw a piece of a fish-box on to the flames. The bowl on the sideboard was heaped with apples, grapes, oranges, bananas and nuts.

Miss Tait looked *very* happy, sitting in her rocker.

But suddenly she was aware of the faces at the window. She made towards the door. And the silent choristers, clustered outside the window, fled. The girls shrieked! Mary slipped in the snow, and cried in terror.

'Come back!' cried Miss Tait from the open door, and it was as if her voice glowed like a candle and trembled like a bell, through the falling snow, 'I have *a new pound coin* for each of you.'

The choristers returned one by one, with smoking breaths. They stood outside Miss Tait's open door. They sang, *We Three Kings of Orient Are.*

Then one by one they came in and stood by the fire. 'Tommy brought me driftwood,' said Miss Tait. 'Now, who likes oranges?'

Tompkins purred merrily beside the blaze.

The Winter Song

At Graystones I got nothing. They were all in bed. Darkness.
I sang outside, under a dark blue coat of sky with three stars
in it.

> Good to be this buirdly bigging!
> We're a' St Mary's men.
> Fae the steeth-stane to the rigging
> Afore wur Lady.

They slept the year out, good temperance people.

At the old ones', Jonah's and Jess's, I got a glass of ginger beer
and a penny. I put my mouth in this shape and that.

> God bless the gudewife and sae the gudeman
> We're a' St Mary's men
> Dish and table, pot and pan
> Afore wur Lady.

They clapped their hands. Old Jess kissed me. The row of
blue dishes twinkled on the sideboard.

At Peggy's, no luck. Her door was locked. Peggy was visiting
Jock her sweetheart. I sang a verse for the house, all the same,
under a purple one-star robe of sky.

> Where is the gudewife o' this hoose?
> Where is she, that dame?

At Mirran and Tom's, Mirran shook a finger at me. 'Why aren't you with the other boys? I swear, you're the strangest loneliest boy in this island.' I sang a verse, my voice shaking. Mirran has a sharp tongue.

> Gudeman, go to your brewing vat
> And fetch us here a quart o' that

Mirran gave me the thickest piece of gingerbread I had ever blocked my mouth on. The magic of winter was in that gingerbread. It glowed in my belly. 'Well sung,' said Tom. Mirran pinched her thin face into a smile.

At Tofthouse, the dog set up, when I'd knocked, the blackest barking! Nobody opened the door. There had been a death in that place in November: Rachel who made the butter and lit the fires.

> Whar is the servant lass o' this hoose?
> Whar is she, that lass?

I set my small song against the black mouth of Faithful the dog.

At old Sillock's, sixpence – it shone between my fingers like a star! Two verses I gave the grey fisherman.

> King Henry he is no at hame
> But he is to the greenwids gane

He had taken the coin from a bottle at the back of the bed, like an old pirate king who has been in far perilous places and gives rich rewards.

At Billtock's, nothing. Billtock had been taken away to the poorhouse after harvest. Now a stone has fallen from the roof. I whispered a few words of the song into the rusty keyhole.

> May a' your hens rin in a reel,
> And every ane twal' at her heel

Son of Billtock, come back soon from Australia. The heart of the house is, now, a cold black hearth. The hen-house is a cluster of wet boards.

At Nessvoe, Willie and Jessie set me in their great straw chair, legs dangling. Willie looked at me solemnly through owl spectacles (price of one shilling from the wandering hawker). Jessie gave me a cup of ale. I sang till the cups on Jessie's dresser shivered. The ale had made me reckless and gay. I uttered all kinds of blessing, half the song.

> May a' your kye be weel to calf
> And every ane hae a queyo calf
>
> May a' your mares be weel to foal
> And every ane hae a mare foal
>
> May a' your yowes be weel to lamb
> And every ane hae a yowe and a ram . . .

'That's not likely,' said Willie, and he eyed me like a friendly owl.

*   *   *

At the sea-captain's, nothing. 'Impudent little wretch! Begging, is it? Does your mother know you're out in the dark night begging? A disgrace. That nonsense of a song, January after January – I'm sick of it! . . . Go away, boy. I'm poor. I have nothing for you. I've navigated a hundred seas to come home and get some peace at last. I don't have sovereigns in a teapot under the stair – all lies, nonsense. Impudent little pirate that you are . . . That wind's blowing off Iceland. You best hurry off home, pirate. There's a gale and a blizzard coming.'

> We hae wur ships sailan the sea
> And mighty men o'lands are we

I sang to the wharf-bound miserable rotting hulk of a house.

Andrew and Annie are just newly married in a new house, Rosevale. I sang,

> This night is good New 'ar ev'n's night
> And we've come here to claim wur right
> Goodwife, go to your butter ark
> And weigh us oot o' that ten mark

Andrew and Annie laughed. 'A bairn's blessing on a new fire and bed – what better?' They gave me what was left of the wedding largesse, the squandered 'boys ba'' – one penny and four ha' pennies and three farthings. I stayed so long at their leaping fire, the load of money in my pocket burned through to my thigh. Annie bade me 'A Good New Year!' Her voice rang like a bell under the frosty lintel.

*   *   *

On the hillside, a star or a snowflake fell cold on my nose. I heard, on the far side of the hill, the horde of village boys going with their threatening chorus.

> Be ye maids or be ye nane
> Ye's a' be kissed or we gang hame
> If you dunno open your door
> We'll lay it flat upon the floor

'I hope they don't meet me!' Silver moths fell and folded on my shivering cheek and fingers.

At Norbreck, nothing. Sander lives alone. He's deaf. He goes to bed early. What good's a song to a deaf widowed wall-facer? I sang. Flakes fluttered on to his window, a silver host.

> If we get no what we seek
> We'll tak' the head o' your Yule sheep

Sander slept, dreaming of flocks and a bonny fireside spinner long dust.

Near the Glebe, I fell in the ditch. The singing horde of boys went past, with flake-dark lanterns, a field away. I sang, all slush and blue bruises, to the twelve whisky drinkers in the Glebe. One of them offered me his flask. I filled my mouth with flames and glory and the richness of furrows.

> And the three-legged cog that's standing fu'
> Fetch it here to weet wur mou'

> This is the best that we can tak'
> And we will drink till wur lugs crack

A fiddle struck up. An eightsome reel went round, with Cherokee yells.

I stood, a boy of stars, at the laird's gate. The gentry did not hear me. Inside, bunches of candles, broken ceiling lights from a bell made of crystal pieces that collided and made tiny music. Mirrors glooming and softly gleaming. Mr Sweyn the laird would be nodding in his oak chair between the flames and the decanter. His silver-haired lady sat opposite sewing an alphabet on a sampler. They do not hear a small fist on the mighty ancient door panels of the Hall.

> Good be tae this buirdly bigging
>   We're a' St Mary's men
> Fae the steethe-stane tae the rigging
>   Afore wur Lady

Hall or hovel, don't the doors and windows and chimneys need as much blessing as they can get, always? 'We're poor things, even at the best,' my grandfather would say, sadly and wonderingly, when word would come to the island of the death of a prince or a millionaire.

My pocket rang like a bell, going shorewards. I heaved home, a pirate ship blizzard-borne between black sky and eerie-white glimmering earth. I dipped home with a cargo of coins and stars.

And my mother cried in the open door, 'Where have you been? What a sight, filth from eyes to feet! Snow in your hair! Your supper's cold' . . . The baby cried from the cradle. Granda nodded over by the fire. Stars whirled past my shoulder on to the blue stone floor. My mother put a kiss on my cheek, a sweet red warm star. Granda, sipping his Hogmanay toddy, grumbled at a sudden blown star-swirling coldness upon the knees and hands of his last winter.

My mother closed the door. Our fire flamed like the sun. I ate a hot buttered bannock. The croft was a little secure summer in the heart of perpetual snow. My mother sang to the child. I nodded off to sleep, my head like a bee-hive.

Dialogue at the Year's End

'I've been out all this short day,' said the old cripple woman in the straw chair by the fire. 'I was keeping the ways clear between the house and the barn and the byre and the stable. I shovelled and shovelled till the snow stood higher than myself. Sometimes I was half blinded with the brightness.' 'If you aren't a wonder,' said the apple-faced child in the door.

'What can anybody do in February?' said the old done woman with the grey shawl muffling her mouth. 'Oh but my needles went clickety-clack, clickety-clack, and a jumper with bonny patterns brown and white fell from the knitting needles. I'll be the bonniest lass at the barn dance at the Bu come the weekend. I will.'

'No gull was ever so busy,' said the flame-bright boy, and put another peat on the fire.

'Oh,' said the old wife on two sticks, 'they're the lazy ones, men. A bit of a blow from the west, a wave or two clashing on the shore, and it's too stormy for the sea. *Up and off with you*, I cried this morning, *there's a thousand cod off Yesnaby* . . . The one that's to be my man come harvest, he was the first to push out. The *Gannet*, that's the name of his boat. They followed, one after another. By sunset today I was gutting a hundred fish.'

'This place would starve without you,' said the grass-green boy.

*   *   *

'I'm always one to keep a bonny house,' said the old grannie in a voice like withered grass. 'So after porridge time, I found seven stone jars in the cupboard. Ah, it was bonny today on the hill. I came home with my apron brimming with buttercups and daisies and long sweet grasses. I filled the jars and I sent them here and there about the house. I took the loan of daffodils from the grieve's garden. The daffodils I put in water in a jar in the window.'

'You make everything bright that you touch,' said the child with flower-sweet skin.

'I forget what I did today,' said the old dame with chin whiskers. 'I'm beginning to forget things. Oh now I know – I made ale. I steeped a hundredweight of malt and I threw in brown sugar, handful on handful, and I added the barm. And oh! I nearly forgot – I poured in a jar of honey. There will never be a more noble head of froth in this island, never, nowhere. There's a hundred reels and dances in that ale. It will drive the fiddlers mad. Men will tell stories about this brew of mine. It's to be for a certain wedding.'

'This island is happy for you alone,' said the boy with lochblue eyes.

'Well, what a day this has been!' said she of the toothless mouth. 'We gathered the kindling all week. We went in one long line, with loaded shoulders up the hill. We poured in fat and fish oil. At midnight the laird lit the fire – his face was red with port wine and flames. Fifty young shadows sang and danced through the flames. At sunrise, even the jealous ones agreed, I and a certain boy were the best pair of dancers round the midsummer fire.'

'I hope he kissed you,' said the child with a white butterfly in his fingers.

*   *   *

'A day is so short,' said the old wife with cindery breath. 'I think I waited at some grand table today, candles and bottles of wine and a silver plate with salmon and a silver plate with grouse. But was it the Manse or the Hall or the Hamnavoe provost's house? Wherever it was, a fine man said across his wineglass, *Everything tastes sweeter because of the waitress.* Hanks of cigar-smoke hung over the table. I wouldn't change my fisherman for him, gold watch-chain and cigar and fine high chant.'

'You're better than any lady in London,' said the boy with honey strands between his fingers.

'I can't talk of tiredness,' said the rattle of bone-and-stick from the rocking-chair. 'I think I was never so tired. My body is veined with the heavy gold of harvest. From rise of sun to rose of sunset we laboured. I followed the flame and flash of a certain scythe, I bent and I bound the scatterings of gold like Ruth. The corncrakes creaked. The bees trudged home with their own pure gold. At noon the women poured bottles of ale in a jug, and they spread bannocks with golden butter. One young harvester snored against a stook, his head humming like a hive. I shook him awake, but gently.'

'You're the golden girl,' said the child with the ear of corn twined in his hair.

'Oh this, this,' said the old dreamer, her face laved in flame-shadows, 'this was the very happiest day of my life. First thing, I washed in sweet cold water. Then the girls swathed me about in a heavy whiteness. Then we followed the fiddler, a long long column, from my father's croft to the kirk. The minister came with his book and we stood before him, the man and me, and he put the gold ring on my shivering finger – look. Then we followed the fiddle home. The man threw pennies to the parish boys. The world came to the wedding – the cows and the horses, the grass and the clouds and the waves, the sun followed us in through the door, and when I looked through the skylight, the stars had come to the wedding, and the moon put silver coins on the loch for the wedding. Where are you now? Why don't you speak to me, man?'

'A stone is generally silent,' said the boy with the blackbird breath.

'The silence was hardest of all to bear,' sighed the old woman with webs at her mouth. 'Today the silence crushed me like quernstones. That silence box-long on the trestles. Then the figures in black one by one coming to my chair, and pausing, and going on out. The silence borne away by eight black silences. Then the black silent shawls of the neighbours about me, in a slow dark silent dance, all day. The last one lit the lamp and left. Silent they drifted across the pane, first snowflakes. I woke in this chair by the dead fire. The room was bright with snow and dawn.'

'The swan's silent too,' cried the silver voice of the child beside the snowman.

'I was never so happy and never so tired,' cried the swan princess, flying between the hill and the loch with a sun-cake in its beak. 'Where must I fly with this sun-cake? I took it from the hand of a boy who stood in a poor croft door, it was yellow with barley and honey, it was warm from peatsmoke and flame. Where should I take the sun-cake that is baked on the hearth in the depths of winter, when the wick of the sun burns low and cold in the south? My wings are heavy, the loch is frozen over.'

'To the poorest house in the world,' chimed the crystal in the throat of the child. 'Go out, old grandmother, now through the snow, with the suncakes in your basket.'

A Croft in January

'You stay indoors,' said the boy's mother, a new widow. 'Sit over there beside the fire. Read a book. This is the most treacherous time of the year, January. I don't want any more illness in this house. I'll put another peat on the fire. There's a good boy. I'll just be back from the byre.'

As soon as his mother went to milk the cow, the boy was out and away.

Oh, it was bleak all right! The Hogmanay snow was shrinking. It had been beautiful while it lay like a white quilt over the island, under the full moon. But now the snow had shrunk to tattered rags of grey along the dykes and on the hill-top.

As he came round the corner, the wind cut into him like a scythe.

He ran towards the village. The melting snow on the road seeped into his boots and he felt his feet cold. Thin spits of rain came out of the grey sky . . . This was better, though, than the grief and the silence of the fatherless croft.

In the first days after New Year – after the first-footing and the whisky bottles and the singing of the old midwinter song in every croft – the village seemed always to shrink into itself and batten down for the worst of winter. For, as the old folk said, 'as the day lengthens the caald strengthens' . . .

The length of the village, there was nobody to be seen. The boy peeked in at the inn door. The fire was burning for nobody. John Baillie the inn-keeper was playing patience on the dry counter. Where, this afternoon, were all the merry men of recent days, with their red faces and loud mouths and bottles of whisky sticking out of their pockets? Where were the miller, the blacksmith, the three fishermen, the seven crofters, the shepherd, the ferryman? They were crouched, wretched and penniless, over the fires here and there – and the tongues of womenfolk making their hangovers more wretched.

The thought of his father came to the boy. Well, he was beyond songs and ale-house fires and hangovers now. And his mother was more silent than ever she had been, except when she broke out in complainings.

'Your brother should be here, him that emigrated to Australia ten years ago. Your father might have died quiet then. This croft has been in the one family for seven generations. The way things are, it's the poor-house for you and me, boy. I don't want their charity. There was Willa of Taing here last night when you were sleeping, with eggs and oat-cakes. I sent her about her business.'

The sun was down. He saw the postman going with his lantern and bag across the hill.

He had one penny in his pocket. Oh, he was glad to see that the shop was open. It had been closed since Hogmanay.

He went inside. Sandra, the general merchant, had no customers either. She looked up from her Fair-Isle knitting. 'A pennyworth of pandrops,' said the boy.

'You're all blue and shivering,' said Sandra. 'It's no weather for a boy like you to be out. I'm surprised your mother let you over the door.'

She tilted a white rattling rush of pandrops from the jar on the counter into a white paper poke.

'It'll be a poor year up at Svendale, this,' said Sandra. 'I think a pity of your poor mother. Who's going to plough your field this February? It's a hard thing when the bread-winner's taken.'

Sandra put the poke of sweeties on the counter. The boy put his last penny on the counter.

'No no,' said Sandra. 'You keep your penny. This is a present for you.'

'I don't want charity,' said the boy. He picked up the sweetie-bag and left the shop.

'Always a proud lot up at Svendale,' he heard the old shop-wife saying as the door pinged behind him.

The village lay like a grey corpse under the first darkness. A star flickered like a candle between two urgent clouds.

The boy had never known such desolation. The year was dead, the village was dead, the shutters of destitution would be nailed across the windows of their croft in the month of May, when there was no money to meet the rent.

Ah, there was a third lighted door in the village! Willie Learmonth the fisherman was alive, thank goodness.

The pools along the village street were beginning to freeze over. He almost slipped and fell, crossing over to the boatshed above the shore. He opened Willie's door without knocking. Willie was sitting over by the stove baiting his lines beside the paraffin lamp. 'If it isn't Thorfinn!' he cried. 'A happy New Year, Thorfinn. Come over by the stove and warm you.'

'Where's Tom and Andrew?' said the boy.

'They're still recovering from Hogmanay,' said the fisherman. 'Somebody must work. So here I am. I have no wife to rage at me, I'm thankful to say.'

'Please, Willie,' said the boy, 'I'd be very pleased if you'd sign me on soon. I've always wanted to be a fisherman with you on the *Venture*. I don't like farming.'

Willie the fisherman eyed him gravely. 'Well,' said he, 'maybe after summer – or the spring after that. You need a bit more muscle and bone on you. I'll be glad for you to be on the *Venture* then.'

'I see,' said the boy.

'Look,' said Willie. 'I have some salted ling in the rafters. Take some home to your mother. Wish her, from me, a better year than she had last year, poor soul.'

'We don't take charity,' said the boy.

When the boy got home, slithering on the ice, he expected no less a tongue-lashing than the hung-over New Year celebrants had gotten from their woman-folk on January the second.

But his mother was in her chair with the lamp-light on her face and a paper in her hand. The postman had called. 'A letter from your brother in Australia. Fancy that, after ten years! A sheep farmer, that's what he is. And look at this!' . . . He read, by the firelight, a postal draft for ten pounds.

'This'll pay the rent and plenty to spare,' said his mother. 'We can keep the cow. I can even buy two sheep and a flock of hens. Our furniture won't be set on the road outside, in May. Some folk will be disappointed, I dare say'.

'I have news too,' said the boy. 'Willie Learmonth of the *Venture* is taking me on for a fisherman.'

The Weaver

This is a busy time for me. Now, in tempest and blizzard, is a busy time always. *Make a length of cloth, man, hurry.* Or, *Even at the fire, inside, we are cold . . .* No lack of business now. I set the shuttle flying, the grey weave grows in the loom. But when they come for the cloth, no silver shines in their hands. *You'll be paid at egg-time, in April . . . The harvest in, there'll be a shilling or two.*

I have a second loom, empty. I dream, in an idle hour, of the beauty and richness I would cast upon that loom.

The coats of the fishermen are never dry. Let them hang in wind and sun, the spindrift is so worked into the coats of fishermen that they are heavy with salt always.

The skipper of *Tern* knocks. He stands in the door. He comes in. He can hardly see in the gloom and peat-smoke. *I need a thick sea coat, man. The salt has eaten my old coat.*

If I saw the glint of a shilling, it might give me the strength to weave, I say.

The door opens. A boy lays a bunch of haddocks on my stone floor. The skipper's boy.

The sea, outside my window, is a fleece of foam.

The second loom is empty, still. Some day it will hold a web of splendour.

My stock of yarn is low. I must go to the crofts where the spinning-women sit at their fires. One by one, they put their cold hard looks on me. There was one girl, long ago – her sweetness is gone like the gleam of snow.

Here comes the old miser, the weaver, a child cries at an open door.

A dozen croft-wives will spin for me before the end of April. I have their promises.

One pauses, her hand on the wheel.

Ploughmen are out in every field, making furrow on furrow. None greets me. None wears a coat. It is a hot heavy toil, ploughing.

For that lost young face, my hands might have wrought good images on the empty loom.

I can't abide to be outdoors, in April. The new light dazzles me. The bright lambs, ditches spilling daffodils, the kindling sun, the sea-gleams near and far.

How glad I am to keep indoors, going between the web and the loom.

One woman brings milk. One woman brings bread or fish. One woman brings a bucket of water from the burn. They lift the penny I leave on the doorstep, under three stones.

My loft is well stocked with yarn for the weaving. Every year, a bird breaks through the roof, bears some wool away for its nest.

I fall asleep over the loom, over a half finished stretch.

I waken. A small girl from the next croft is putting a jar of daffodils on my window-sill.

She goes away without a word. I don't even know her name.

By daffodil-light, I see a score of spider-webs and the greyness of my cloth and the empty loom in the corner.

A big ship anchors off the island. The tall foreign skipper consults with fishermen on the shore. The fishermen point to my house.

I hear you are the famous weaver in this island.

I don't let the man over the threshold.

I am a weaver, I say.

I am told, you are a maker of very beautiful cloths, he says.

I make grey lengths for crofters and fisherman, I say. *Nothing more.*

But your great skills are known in Bergen and Lubeck, he says.

Once, in my youth, I tell him, *I made more than grey cloths. But the light left me, suddenly, long ago, and I no longer make the beautiful cloths you have heard of.*

The tall foreigner does not understand what I mean. *Go into the kirkyard,* I say, *on your way to the shore and the ship. There you'll see a stone with INGA of GARTH carved on it.*

Still he seems not to understand.

I would like to take home to my wife in Norway such a fine web of cloth as once you made.

There is a purse in his hand. I warrant it is well stuffed with crowns and doubloons.

I open the door wider. I point to the empty loom. *Look there,* I say.

Then I close the door against him.

Bale on bale of cloth, in the long days of mid-summer. I stack the bales in my attic. They do not need the cloth now, they are busy with their peat-cutting and fishing. The women make abundance of butter and cheese. The men visit the green corn-patches twice a day, anxiously. Children go like clouds across the hill.

In the first chill of September, there will be beatings on my door. The women from the big farm: *Be sure to have cloth enough for two big coats and five small coats* . . .

I climb the ladder to the attic with a new bale.

The rats have been at my work! The rats and the moths have been devouring here and there. Three bales of cloth are ruined! How shall I live through the winter?

I climb down. I put my head on the empty loom. I dream of an impossible incorruptible beauty.

Those summer storms fall on chartless ships and drive them here and there, rudderless, against reef and crag.

Last night, for hours, lanterns thronged clifftop and shore. There are hold-plunderings in plenty when a ship is wrecked. The wild hands of the sea can throw anything about their feet – casks of rum, apple barrels, bales of cotton. Then the islanders huddle the cargoes away, before the excise men come. They have their hiding places.

I light my lantern and go down at midnight. I have a wild hope: it might be a cargo of English wool.

I have to laugh at the long faces at the shore. It is a poor ship, *Erin*, out of Galway, carrying a troop of entertainers to the Low Countries, itinerant musicians and verse-men.

Their only cargo a few harps and flutes and masks.

And the wretches of play-actors huddle there under the cliff, all shaking and grey-mouthed.

Had *Erin* been a lordly ship, they would have lain that night at the laird's fire. But nobody wanted such outcasts: penniless rootless rogues.

The blacksmith says it's warm enough at his forge. They can all lie there till morning.

One street-singer follows my lantern. *I can see you're a man of talent like myself*, says he. *I'd sing you the loveliest ballad ever made, only my harp's drowned.*

I stoke up the fire and put cheese and bread and a cup of ale in his hands. He crosses himself and lies down to sleep at the fire.

I dream: my empty loom is a harp, a young king is weaving golden music there, and when it is finished he takes the coat-of-songs from the harp and puts it on and goes out to be with princes and lords, in a great hall far away.

A fishing boat takes them to Scotland in the morning.

I give the singer an old coat to wear, that he might not die of cold before he gets home to his green hills. I wore it when I was an apprentice and went to dances and fairs.

A young man is shearing the twenty sheep of Garth.

The sheep of Garth have good fleeces.

A child shouts, *Here he comes, old Clack-clack the weaver.*

Sheep run here and there, bewildered with lightness and cold.

I've seen better fleeces, I say to the young shearer. (I say these words every year.)

The man lets on never to hear me.

It is beautiful wool. It is too good for the coats of peasants and fishermen. The laird might wear such cloth to his council meetings in Kirkwall or to his receptions in the Canongate of Edinburgh. Oh no – it is far too fine for the likes of him, even.

I rub a curl of fleece between thumb and finger. Oil-of-wool gleams. It is the best wool for years.

Why is the man of Garth not shearing his own sheep? I say.

The young man wrestles another sheep over on the hill.

He is sick, he says. *He's been sick since the shipwreck.*

The father of a dead girl is sick. The man of Garth must be very old now. There is a time to wither . . .

It is wool of such purity, it ought to be spun by women's hands for a new bride. My workaday loom is too coarse.

Tell the man of Garth I wish him well.

*　　*　　*

I have this strange gift, that I can see in the face of any woman its end and its beginning.

Once only I saw a face that seemed to have the light of noon and of summer on it always. (But only a stone keeps such endurings.)

All the islanders are kin. You can see a glance or a gesture that has drifted through generations.

It is so long since I mingled with them that I forget names and places.

An old woman knocks. *I'm sent to bid you to the Harvest Home.*

Through the webs and wrinkles I see a face that pierces me. It is a girl that stands there, with a sweet summons to the ale-kirn and the fiddles, in a barn, under the arch of stars.

I am a weaver. It'll soon be winter. I must work.

At once she is an old hag, shaking her head, all sourness. I clash the door against her.

Another morning, it is a flutter at the door. It must, I think, be a bird at the doorstep.

No, it is a small girl. *Hurry*, she cries, *the boat's leaving for the Lammas Fair.*

I see in her the old withered woman. I have pity for the child. She turns from the blackbird, she looks at me with a look that has drifted down generations, the glance that has sweetened the labour of this island from the beginning, and made all worthwhile, ploughtime and net-splurge and harvest, even the drownings and the burnings. She is the one who summoned me, once, long ago.

I'm the weaver, I cry. *I have to make cloth for all the crofters and fishermen.*

I have a jar with coins on the mantelpiece.

I give the child a sixpence to take to the Fair.

*   *   *

In October, grey airs move about the house. This October, I feel the draughts keenly. It is time to light the fire.

Why are there no peats stacked at the end of the house? The young crofter of Glebe leaves a cartload of peat at my door every autumn.

Ah, I know why it is. His young wife was at my door before harvest. *That bale of cloth you sent up to Glebe last week,* says she, *it was poor stuff, it was so thin here and there you could see through it. Take it back.*

Well, says I, *there'll be many a one glad of it before New Year, madame . . .* Off she goes with a fling of the head.

What will I do for a fire tonight?

There's that loom that's lying there useless. Look, it's all warped. It'll never work again! That'll keep you in fire for a night or two.

But when I take the axe to smash the loom, I can't do it.

I lay down my head on the empty loom.

Why is the frame wet?

Cold shakes wetness from the eyes of an old man.

There's a man who makes more lasting clothes than me – the undertaker. (I forget his name too.)

He comes to my door at night, in the first brief snow of November.

The old man of Garth died at sunset, says he.

That's your business, says I.

No, but they want a shroud. They've searched Garth high and low and there's no shroud for him. They want everything done decently.

I could have told him who was wrapped in that shroud.

They'll have their shroud in the morning, I tell him of the red cheeks and lugubrious eyes.

I am up all night making a shroud for the good old crofter of Garth.

I think to myself, *This snow will take them in a troop to my door. I make my living from winter and the fear of kirkyards.*

It snowed all night. The air crackled with frost.

Where is the woman with my bowl of milk? Where is the woman with my bucket of water? Where is the woman with my loaf?

The three pennies are lost under snow on the doorstep. That is why the women have passed me by.

At least I will break the ice in the burn and get water.

The brightness of sun on snow cuts my eyes like a knife.

There they are, at the end of the house, in a cackle of gossip. They are on their way with the milk, the bread, the water.

Oh, says the water-carrier, *it's true. In the ruins of Quoy. I saw a light in the window last night.*

A man and a girl, says the baker of bread. *Strangers.*

The inn couldn't take them, says the cheese wife. *For one thing, they had no money.*

But that isn't all, they seemed to say all together, like a chorus. *There's a child, a new-born infant.*

I leave them to their palaver. They are on their way to my door. Who has come this midwinter to live in the ruin of Quoy is not my business.

I open the door. A weave beyond the light of snow lies, fold on fold, across the loom that had lain useless for fifty winters.

I look through my window. The snow is grey. I see the three women going across the fields to Quoy, carrying the water, the butter, and the bread.